The Sheriff
and the
Folsom Man Murders

Previous "Sheriff" novels by D. R. Meredith

The Sheriff and the Branding Iron Murders
The Sheriff and the Panhandle Murders

The Sheriff
and the
Folsom Man Murders

D. R. Meredith

Walker and Company
New York

First published in the United States of America in 1987 by the Walker Publishing Company, Inc.

Published simultaneously in Canada by John Wiley & Sons Canada, Limited, Rexdale, Ontario.

Library of Congress Cataloging-in-Publication Data

Meredith, D. R. (Doris R.)
    The sheriff and the Folsom man murders.
    I. Title.
PS3563.E7355S484   1987   813'.54   86-15851
ISBN 0-8027-5663-8

Book design by Teresa M. Carboni

Printed in the United States of America

10 9 8 7 6 5 4 3 2 1

To my own Norwegian friends,
the Nysteuns,
who should
have been born in Texas

ACKNOWLEDGMENTS

Alvin Lynn for his patience in answering all my questions on archeology; Sheriff Andres Cordova and the Union County Sheriff's Department; Sheriff Buck Weaver and the Moore County Sheriff's Department; David Hawkins, who once again shared his knowledge of firearms with an author who doesn't own one; the Federal Bureau of Investigation; and the park rangers at Capulin Mountain National Monument.

The Sheriff
and the
Folsom Man Murders

1

THE GATE WAS locked, but they wouldn't have used it had it been open. Outcasts seldom do. They prefer to slink furtively through the back door, heads bowed and eyes averted, as if to avoid the notice of more respectable citizenry. Not that there were any around. The nearest town, a tiny hamlet of less than a hundred people, was three miles away. The natural guardians, the park rangers, were very comfortably at home in their cinder-block houses behind the visitor center. And why shouldn't they be? Who could steal an extinct volcano, rising one thousand five hundred feet above the surrounding plain, approximately one mile in circumference and with a crater four hundred and fifteen feet deep?

But they didn't come to steal it, only to worship it.

The crouching man shivered and tucked his hands underneath his armpits. It was cold, perhaps more so when one contrasted the frigid air to the fierce heat that had formed the crater long ago. *Surely a matter of several thousand degrees between the two temperatures,* he thought idly. He wondered if the pitiful misfits below him were aware that seven thousand years ago their flesh would have melted, their bones turned to ash, had they dared to enter the crater. Provided they'd lived long enough to even reach the crater. Which they wouldn't have. They would have vaporized beneath the molten lava that flowed from its western base, or suffocated beneath a layer of ash and cinder during its last eruption.

They were really quite contemptible, he decided; a small group of ill-nourished, unclean specimens of some unidentified subgroup of Homo sapiens. He smiled. But interesting, nonetheless, in the same way that any subgroup of a species is interesting.

He shifted uncomfortably and wished he'd worn two pairs of socks. It was damn cold for October, and the forecast had hinted at snow. How did those people stay warm wearing nothing but animal hides? And stiff, poorly tanned hides at that. The whole group of them crackled like potato chips when they walked. They were ridiculous, insignificant nonentities. All but one.

He focused on the one—a tall, bare chested man—and resentment curled his hands into fists. The Leader! A dirty creature with bare feet! And he'd dared to interfere. The girl had very little to do with his reasons for retaliation, of course. She was a convenience, nothing else; certainly not worth fighting about. It was the principle involved. He, Enrique Armijo, did not intend to allow an uncouth savage to dictate his actions.

It wasn't difficult to distinguish her from the others. Her hair was long and blond and, by contrast, reasonably clean. Not an easy accomplishment considering the primitive conditions in which she lived. He'd insisted on cleanliness, but there was also a natural fastidiousness about her, a sort of innate delicacy, that had prevented her from sinking into the same morass of filth as her fellows. One could even say the nasty little surprise he had planned for the Leader was to her benefit. He was saving a lovely flower from a dung heap.

He smiled at his metaphor. He might even assist in her transplanting. Properly dressed, she would be fit to accompany him to certain functions, those that did not require her to converse. Which meant she'd never see the inside of Dr. Hagan's old adobe house. For himself, he seldom required conversation from his women, but the chairman of the archeology department seemed to think intelligent women were an asset to a dinner party. It was one of the many topics about which he and Dr. Hagan disagreed.

Dr. Hagan, he thought with his usual frustration, *would enjoy the ritual being performed by these pseudo-primitives.* He would probably even borrow a half-rotten antelope skin and join the circle squatting around the tiny fire. He could almost see the professor's Buddha-like body swaying to the tempo of the soft, monotonous chant.

His eyes snapped open, and he felt disoriented. A light, almost nonexistent, mist was falling, and for a moment it seemed as if it were steam rising from the crater itself. He half rose and strangled back a cry of superstitious horror. The figures around the fire had shrunk into brutish shapes with coarse matted hair and broad flat feet. The jagged boulders of solidified lava that choked the original vent of the volcano were pulsating with hot molten light. The Gambel oak and mountain mahogany, the pinyon and skunkbush, the juniper and chokecherry, disappeared, and the walls of the crater rose behind and in front and on all sides of him; their cinder and ash structure unblemished by vegetation.

Blindly his hands came up, palms out in a defensive gesture as old as the first creature who walked upright. He twisted around to escape and slammed one thigh against a prickly pear. Hundreds of fine little needles pierced his denim jeans and embedded themselves in his flesh.

With an inarticulate cry he sprawled forward away from the cactus and brushed at his leg. Needles barely caught in the denim eagerly found a more secure home in his hand. Leg and hand burning and stinging, he struggled upright, his face twisted with equal measures

3

of pain and fury. Any Celt in old Britain would have recognized his expression as that of a berserker, a man crazed with bloodlust, ready to rush into the midst of his enemies and kill and kill and kill. But he wasn't a Viking bent on murder; he was a Latin who prided himself on logic. Revenge was a cold emotion, a matter of rational planning and careful execution. And he was a scientist, a very meticulous man.

Drawing a sobbing breath, he looked down toward the fire. There was an explanation for his behavior. He had simply allowed himself to become hypnotized by the tuneless chant. *Plus some drug thrown into the fire,* he thought. The Leader must use a hallucinogen to alter his followers' perception of reality. That was no reason for anger; charlatans of every age had used trickery to maintain their power. Unfortunately he had been close enough to be affected, too.

Shuddering at the thought of what might have happened if he had not rubbed against the cactus plant, he searched for the Leader's tall figure. His eyes were blurring, and he wiped them on his coat sleeve. He was crying from pain and the humiliation of it was greater than any he had ever suffered. Tears were for women and weaklings. Enrique Armijo was above such emotionalism. Enrique Armijo did not allow his superiority to the common herd to be threatened in this way.

Blinking fiercely, he peered again at the fire and the creatures around it. He stiffened, shocked at whom he saw, or rather, did not see. He felt the back of his neck tingle in primeval response, and still crouching, turned awkwardly. He heard it first and recognized the sound for what it was. Not many men would have, but then not many men had his scope of knowledge. He was brilliant after all, the best in his field.

He felt it first as a tremendous pressure on his chest, then as an explosion of pain. In the split second before

4

he died, he admitted the irony of his own death. But then, he was a man who appreciated irony.

The murderer stood without moving for several minutes. He seemed to be able to hear his own heartbeat, but decided it was his imagination. He was trembling, however, and his chest was heaving as if he were a long distance runner. Killing wasn't easy; particularly for someone who had never done it before. He hadn't expected the physical weakness, the queasiness, the perspiration that soaked his forehead and ran in tiny rivulets down his chest. He wondered if he had the physical strength to do what still must be done.

He forced himself to move toward the body until he stood over it, and he marveled that Enrique Armijo seemed so much smaller dead than alive. He smiled wryly at himself. He shouldn't be surprised. It was only poetic justice that Enrique Armijo's physical remains matched his soul. Provided the man had possessed one, which was doubtful.

Hearing a rustling among the Gambel oak shrubs that grew like weeds on the slopes of the crater, he jerked around, his eyes searching uselessly in the darkness. He shivered from the chill air moving across his sweat-soaked body and realized he was afraid. Not of Enrique's uneasy spirit, but of being captured. He most emphatically didn't want to be caught, certainly not for murdering a man like Armijo.

Unable to see a shadow, nor feel a presence that didn't belong, he turned back and glanced toward the fire. He wasn't afraid of those swaying figures lost in some vision of their own making. They had seen nothing and would see nothing until released from their trance. He was safe except from his own conscience. He hadn't really expected to feel any guilt. Relief, yes; but not this feeling of having done something shameful. The man had asked to be killed. There were some people like that, people so insensitive and cruel they deserved killing. He would have to learn to live with guilt. He certainly didn't intend to run to the nearest sheriff and confess just so he'd feel better.

Grasping the wooden shaft, he pulled. The weapon remained stationary, and he panicked. Placing his foot on the corpse's chest to gain more leverage, he jerked harder. Sweat was trickling into his eyes, making them burn. Desperate now, he jerked again, frantic to escape. The shaft came free and he staggered, off balance for a moment. Recovering, he stood panting for breath and glanced at what he held in his hands. It was rounded, about an inch in diameter, and between four and five feet in length. But it was bare of the projectile point that had been attached to it. He wanted to scream and shake his fist at the sky, to curse God, anything to relieve his frustration. Instead he forced himself to think. There was no way of retrieving the foreshaft of the dart with its projectile point, other than mutilating the body, and he couldn't do that. Besides, there was nothing distinctive about the flint point fastened with sinew to the end of the foreshaft. Several of them, erroneously labeled arrowheads, had been collecting dust in homes around this area for nearly a hundred years. And he'd be willing to bet half the people with access to a so-called arrowhead had a motive to murder Enrique Armijo.

2

SHERIFF CHARLES TIMOTHY Matthews leaned back in his chair, with his feet propped comfortably on his desk, and debated whether he wanted to answer the soft knock on his door. He ordinarily wouldn't even be in his office on a Sunday, but with Raul in New Mexico on some vaguely mentioned family business, the sheriff's department was one deputy short. Since he and Meenie Higgins were the only ones without family, they'd elected to work.

Charles smiled. His mother wouldn't appreciate his saying he had no family. But Dallas was several hundred miles south, and it wasn't home anymore. Home was Crawford County: nine hundred square miles of sparsely populated land in the middle of the Texas Panhandle. Instead of diesel fuel and asphalt, the air smelled of growing crops and sagebrush, feedyards and cattle, and the elusive odor of vast, empty land.

The knock was repeated, and he sighed in resignation. It was probably Slim Fletcher. The young deputy was attempting to fill in for Miss Poole as dispatcher. Charles sighed again. Slim's problem was that everything he did was an attempt; his rate of success at anything was damn low.

Might as well get it over with, he thought grimly. One of Slim's few virtues was persistence. "Come in," he called as he laced his hands behind his head and stared patiently at the ceiling. At least that way he would miss his deputy's apologetic expression while he listened to the explanation for whatever fiasco Slim was coming to confess.

"Charles." Angie Lassiter's voice was hesitant and softer than usual.

"Angie!" Charles straightened his six-foot-three-inch frame from its nearly parallel position with the floor, catching his chair before it overturned. He flushed in embarrassment, a condition most of his deputies were unaware he was capable of, and gestured at his desk. "I was just, uh, catching up on a little paperwork."

Angie closed the door and leaned against it. "Am I bothering you? I can come back later." She rubbed her palms on her gold-colored woolen slacks. "No, I can't. I have to talk to you now."

He felt his stomach tighten up as if his body were preparing for physical combat. Angie knew something. Or someone had told her something. Desperately he sought of a way to put off the confrontation he'd been dreading for more than a year. "Where are the girls?" he asked, his voice sounding false to himself. "Didn't you bring them with you?"

"I left our chaperones home with Miss Poole."

"Miss Poole," repeated Charles.

Angie walked over and placed her hands on his chest, then slowly slid them up around his neck and rested her body against him. "Your dispatcher, Charles."

He didn't know which bothered him the most: feeling her against him, which was distracting as hell, or hearing that Miss Poole was involving herself in Angie's life. He didn't distrust the retired school teacher-turned-dispatcher, but he'd learned that like God, Miss Poole moved in mysterious ways. Add to that her conviction that he should tell Angie the truth, and he had good reason to feel as if he'd swallowed live coals.

He stood rigidly in her arms. "I know who she is. I just didn't know you'd become such close friends."

She hesitated a moment, the expression in her wide-set hazel eyes changing from hope to disappointment to determination, then slipped her arms from around his neck and walked toward his desk. "May we sit down?"

"Yes, yes, of course," he said, his uneasiness growing until his skin felt too tight for his body. He angled one of the wooden armchairs and sat down facing her, their knees almost touching.

"Charles?" she asked.

"Hmm?" he answered, noticing the white line of tension that bracketed her mouth and feeling his usual rage that a mouth created for smiling now habitually looked like that of an abused child's.

She raised her left hand and curled a strand of auburn hair around a finger, a nervous gesture he'd seen her make a hundred times before. A jagged streak of white scar tissue marred her ring finger, and he shuddered. He remembered the peaceful cemetery, her cry of pain as she smashed her hand against her husband's gravestone, and his own helplessness as he'd watched her strip off her wedding and engagement rings and grind them beneath her foot. Involuntarily he touched her hand.

She looked up. "It's all right, Charles. It's just a scar."

It was a great deal more than that, he thought as he watched her clasp her right hand over her left, hiding the mark. Wordlessly, he rose and grasped her elbows, pulling her up against him.

"L.D. is dead, Charles. My husband and your best friend is dead. I know he is because I arranged for the funeral and I saw him buried. But sometimes, when I'm with you, I think L.D. must be in the next room. Why, Charles?"

He lifted his hand to press against his stomach as her question caused the familiar pain to ripple through him. His skin felt cold and clammy, and he fought down sudden nausea. *Because I killed him,* he thought numbly.

Maybe I didn't pull the trigger, but I used my power as sheriff to cover up his murder. Now I want his wife, and I feel guilty as hell.

She looked up at him with a bitter expression in her hazel eyes. "Do you feel like you're poaching? Is that it? Or are you still trying to protect him?"

The pain was getting worse, and he thought of the bottle of pills the doctor had prescribed. "No! I'm trying to protect you. Carroll is a small town, Angie. I don't want anyone gossiping about you."

She leaned closer. "Is that why you never take me out unless we take my daughters with us? Is that why you always leave while it's still daylight, then stand around on my front porch until someone sees you? So the neighborhood knows the Widow Lassiter isn't sleeping with the sheriff of Crawford County?"

The pain was intensifying into agony, and he fought to keep standing up when his body was demanding he double over to give it some relief. "Yes!"

She pushed herself away from him. "I don't believe you. You're hiding something about L.D. What was he guilty of that you still need to protect him more than a year after his death? Why was he running away?"

Adrenaline flooded his body like a dash of cold water, speeding up his heartbeat but leaving him weak with relief. She didn't know! She didn't know her dead husband had murdered two people and attempted to murder two more. She didn't know L.D.'s own death was not an accident, but another murder. He didn't consider even for an instant telling her. Better to let her think he was protecting L.D.'s reputation, if the only alternative was to tell her the truth.

"Does it matter? Whatever he did had nothing to do with you. Can't you just accept my word that it doesn't change how we feel about each other?" He knew she wouldn't even before he saw her shake her head.

10

She rubbed the scar on her finger as if trying to erase it. "No," she said as she looked up at him. "Because it does matter. As long as you're hiding something from me, you're keeping L.D. alive. Even after you marry me, you'll always think of me as L.D.'s wife. You won't be making love to me on our wedding night; you'll be committing adultery."

She reached up to grasp his shoulders. "Don't you understand, Charles? I have to know! Otherwise . . . " Her voice faded on a note of desperation.

"Otherwise what?" he asked as his features tightened into the habitual stern mask that hid his emotions.

Her eyes closed for a moment, then opened to reveal an anguish he didn't think he could endure. "Otherwise, I can't marry you, Charles."

3

It was an ordinary door, typical of public buildings built in the thirties, solid wood with a pane of rippled, cloudy glass in the top half. He wondered how long he'd been staring at it. Five minutes? Five hours? He didn't know, didn't care. He'd ceased to care about anything the minute Angie closed that door behind her.

"Damn you, L.D. Lassiter!" he shouted and heaved an ashtray at the inoffensive door. It struck the solid frame and shattered. The door vibrated on its hinges, and a hairline crack appeared in its glass top, neatly dividing the two lines of block letters that spelled out SHERIFF CHARLES TIMOTHY MATTHEWS.

He knew by the sudden and absolute quiet on the other side of his door that he had approximately five seconds to think of a good reason for throwing an ashtray. He revised his estimate to three seconds when Meenie Higgins jerked open the door.

Charles braced himself for whatever pointed comment Meenie might make, but his deputy hardly had time to shift his tobacco out of the way and open his mouth to speak when Slim came barreling through the doorway, awkwardly fumbling for his gun. Charles thought it was fortunate that the young deputy couldn't talk and draw his gun at the same time. Otherwise, he might find his office decorated with bullet holes.

"Sheriff! You all right?" Slim shouted, excitement and concern warring for supremacy on his freckle-splotched face. His disappointment was almost comical

12

when he saw Charles sitting quietly in his chair. "You're not hurt? Nobody shot you?" he asked hopefully.

Meenie shifted his tobacco again, squinted at the broken ashtray, and expelled a long, patient breath. "Did you hear any shots, son?" he asked the younger deputy.

Slim looked around the room, his hand still on his gun. "He might have used a silencer," he suggested.

Meenie looked disgusted. "You been watchin' them cop shows on TV again. Next thing we know you're gonna get one of them shoulder holsters and shoot yourself in the armpit tryin' to draw your gun. Now go bring me a broom."

Slim scratched his head. "What for?"

"The sheriff dropped an ashtray," Meenie said as he grasped Slim's arm, firmly shoved him through the door, and closed it on the young man's face.

Carefully stepping over the broken glass, Meenie walked to the desk, hitched up his western-cut pants, and sat down on one of the wooden armchairs. Without taking his eyes off Charles, he spat into a dented brass spittoon. "Well?" he demanded.

"Well, what?"

"Do you feel any better?"

Charles decided he might as well tell the truth. Meenie Higgins could smell a lie further than most people could smell a skunk. "No," he admitted.

"Didn't think so. You got your hands all curled up into fists like you're lookin' for a fight. Ain't gonna do you no good. L.D. Lassiter's dead."

Charles slammed his clenched fist down on the desk. "Damn it, don't you think I know that?"

"You don't act like it sometimes. Was that what you and Mrs. Lassiter was fightin' about?"

Charles fumbled in his desk drawer for his pills. Unscrewing the lid, he shook two into his hand. "What

Angie and I were discussing has nothing to do with the sheriff's department. . . . "

"You tellin' me to mind my own business?"

Swallowing the pills with what remained of a cold cup of coffee, Charles glared at his deputy. "Weren't you planning to catch up on your paperwork today?"

"What paperwork? Ain't nothin' happened around here except for that Slaughter kid running off the road into old man Bishop's tailwater pit."

"Did you give him a ticket?"

"He was driven' his daddy's brand-new van. By the time I got there, wasn't nothin' showin' but the radio antenna. From what I heard Mr. Slaughter say, that kid ain't gonna be allowed to drive anything but his little brother's Big Wheel 'til he's twenty-five. When you're sixteen, just bein' on foot is punishment enough. I didn't figure he needed a ticket, too."

"Meenie, here's the broom. Want me to sweep up the glass?" Slim stood in the doorway, and Charles was reminded of a puppy anxious to please. Sometimes his young deputy did everything but wag an imaginary tail.

He rose, feeling old and tired and ashamed of himself. "I threw it; I'll clean up the mess."

Slim handed him the broom and dustpan. "How come you threw the ashtray, Sheriff . . . ?" His voice trailed off at the expression on Charles's face, and he made his first mature decision of the day. "I think I better get back to the radio. Never know who might be trying to call in." He backed out the door and gently closed it behind him.

Meenie leaned sideways in his chair and spat in the general direction of the spittoon, again without looking. Involuntarily, Charles's eyes went to the spittoon, but Meenie hadn't missed. The deputy grinned. "You know your problem, Sheriff? You ain't got no faith."

Charles methodically swept the glass onto the dust-

14

pan. "Who are you today? A preacher or a psychologist?"

"I ain't cut out to be one, and I can't spell the other."

"The only words you don't consistently misspell are 'cowboy' and 'Texas,'" observed Charles dryly as he dumped the broken glass into the wastebasket.

"And 'friend,'" said Meenie as he stared at the sheriff from faded blue eyes.

Charles felt his own eyes sting. Turning away, he carefully leaned the broom and dustpan against the wall. Throwing things was enough childish behavior for one day. He didn't need to add tears to the list. His face was its usual stern mask as he sat down and hoisted his feet to the desktop. "Raul's due back tomorrow, so why don't you take the day off?"

Meenie took off his Stetson, pulled a red bandana from his hip pocket, and carefully wiped his forehead. The white band of untanned skin below his hairline gave him a vulnerable look that Charles had never noticed before. Of course he'd only seen Meenie once before without his hat, and that was at a funeral.

Meenie put the hat back on, and the vulnerable look disappeared. He shifted his tobacco and cleared his throat. "You want to talk about it?"

"I thought I told you to mind your own business."

"No, you didn't. You said it wasn't any business of the sheriff's department. That ain't the same thing. Now I'm gonna tell you somethin', and it might make you mad—"

"That's never stopped you before," interrupted Charles.

"—but I been watchin' you, and somebody's goin' to have to straighten you out or that hole in your belly's just gonna get worse 'til you're eat up on the inside. Ever since L.D. was killed you been buildin' a fence around yourself. Last summer when we was out on the Brandin' Iron Ranch solvin' them murders, I thought maybe you

15

was fixin' to take the wire cutters to that fence. You and Mrs. Lassiter was gettin' real close. Then we came back to town, and I could see you startin' to brood again. Last year I wouldn't said nothin'. But things is different. Mrs. Lassiter knows L.D. was runnin' away from somethin'. There ain't no need to protect him anymore."

Charles's feet hit the floor, and he stood up slowly, his face still and hard-looking as he leaned over the desk. "Damn it! I'm not protecting him. I'm protecting Angie!"

"I know it, but there ain't no need. The whole town knows L.D. cleaned out their bank accounts when he left—knew it before she did. She didn't find out 'til the funeral home dunned her for the burial. She had to borrow money from her daddy to pay for it. It's hard to keep mournin' somebody who leaves you flat busted, so she's feelin' guilty instead, wonderin' what she did wrong. She ain't gonna have any peace 'til she know why he was runnin' away. I think you better tell her the truth."

"For what reason? So I could justify violating my oath of office? So she'd see me as a big hero, sacrificing my sacred honor in order to protect her from knowing her husband was a murderer? Damn, don't you understand? She'd feel responsible, because that's the kind of person she is. She'd try to atone for the murders, and the whole damn county would know the truth. She'd ruin her own life and the girls', too. They'd never be able to live down being the daughters of a murderer."

Meenie looked at him and shook his head. "That ain't the only reason. You feel like a murderer yourself. You're afraid to tell her 'cause she might think so, too."

The accusation burrowed its way through his defenses, and he sank weakly back in his chair. "Yes," he whispered. "Not only am I a liar for breaking my oath, but I'm a coward. Now get out of my office. I don't think I can take any more character analysis."

His deputy got up and pushed his hat back on his head.

"You want to know what I think, Sheriff?" he asked as he ambled toward the door.

"No!" shouted Charles.

"I'll tell you anyway. You're the finest man I know. And the biggest damn fool," he added as he hastily escaped through the door.

Charles sat back down and rested his head in his hands. Meenie Higgins believed not only in taking the bull by the horns but twisting his tail at the same time. Damn these Panhandle people. They were too frank, too blunt, too uncompromisingly honest. Hadn't they ever heard of civilized hypocrisy? If a man didn't want to face himself, they shouldn't hold up a mirror.

He got up and walked to the window. The Crawford County sheriff's department was on the third story of the courthouse, and he usually enjoyed looking out over the town. But not today. The courthouse square was empty and bleak-looking. A few remaining leaves on the elms rustled in the ever present Panhandle wind. The grass was the dead, flat yellow of winter. The view was as depressing as his life.

Turning, he restlessly paced his office. If his life was desolate, his own decisions had made it so and he'd stand by them. If that meant giving up Angie in order to protect her, then he'd have to learn to do without her. He rubbed his eyes. He had to get away, to let the wound of losing Angie time to heal. Or perhaps "heal" was the wrong word. "Scar over" was better. Until it became one more scar lost among the others he'd accumulated during his life.

"Sheriff!" Slim was excited. But then he always was. *That's what lack of emotional scar tissue did,* thought Charles bitterly; it left one with the ability to be excited.

"I may be older than you, Slim, but I'm not deaf."

The deputy's forehead wrinkled. "Huh?"

"You're shouting. Unless there's a riot in the jail, a tornado coming, or a shooting, I can't think of a good reason to shout."

Slim's voice dropped a decibel. "Raul's on the phone. He wants to talk to you. He says it's real important."

Charles turned back to the window. "Take his number, and I'll call him back."

"I think you better talk to him, Sheriff." A peculiar note in Meenie's voice forced Charles around. His deputy's leathery skin looked bleached, and he appeared to be in shock. Charles abruptly crossed to his desk and picked up the phone. Anything that could shock Meenie was worth investigating.

"Raul, this is Sheriff Matthews," he said, resting one hip on the edge of his desk. "What did you say to Meenie to scare him so badly? I haven't seen him look so white since that drunk hit him and he swallowed his chewing tobacco." His humor sounded forced even to his own ears.

"I'm in the Clayton, New Mexico, jail"—Raul's voice sounded flat, its usual musical lilt missing—"for murder."

"What?"

"I'm in jail for murder," Raul repeated patiently.

"Raul, don't answer any questions," Charles said urgently. "I'll be there in two hours."

"Don't you want to know who I killed?" asked Raul.

"No, because you didn't kill anyone."

There was a rush of air over the phone as if Raul had been holding his breath for hours. "Thank you."

Charles gripped the phone tighter. "Thanks are not necessary, Raul. Just hang on; I'll be there."

He replaced the receiver and looked up, his expression so forbidding that Slim took a step backward and swallowed the question that had been trembling on his lips.

18

Walking to the coat rack, he carefully removed the leather flap that displayed his badge from his jacket. He looked at it a moment, then looked at his two deputies. "Raul's been arrested for murder."

Meenie shifted his tobacco as he watched Charles lay his badge on the desk. "Yeah, he told me. What are you fixin' to do, Sheriff?" he asked suspiciously.

Charles put on his coat and reached for his Stetson, the only article of Western clothing he ever wore besides his boots. "I'm going to New Mexico to get him out of jail."

"He don't need you; he needs a lawyer."

Charles cocked an eyebrow. "I am a lawyer. Had you forgotten? I have a degree from Southern Methodist University School of Law. I'm a member of the bar association of three states, one of which is New Mexico. Want to see my membership cards?" he asked, pulling out his wallet.

"You got another little card, one that says you're a sheriff. And taking off your badge ain't gonna make you any less of one. You're a Texas sheriff, and you ain't got no business messin' around in New Mexico, especially in old Kit Lindman's stompin' ground. If he catches you, Raul'll have a cell mate."

"Then I'll have to see that he doesn't catch me." Charles smiled and Slim took another step backward. He couldn't understand how a man could smile and look so mean at the same time.

Meenie leaned over and spat in the spittoon. "You're a damn fool, Sheriff."

Charles smiled again. "You're being redundant, Meenie. You've already called me a fool once today."

4

CHARLES HAD NEVER taken a detour through Clayton during any of his trips to the Taos ski basin. Consequently he'd never seen the courthouse, a three-story pressed brick building with a tin roof topped by a cupola, nor met Sheriff Christopher "Kit" Lindman. For his purposes it was just as well. He could hardly masquerade as a lawyer if he were familiar with either the place or the person.

He grimaced at his own thoughts. He was *not* masquerading; he was a lawyer. As a former assistant district attorney in Dallas, and as a sheriff, he was just more used to thinking in terms of prosecution than defense. Theoretically, that should make him a good defense attorney. For Raul's sake, he hoped so.

He parked in a gravel lot behind the courthouse and got out of the car. He shivered in the thin air. Clayton was more than a thousand feet higher in altitude than Crawford County, and the temperature was decidedly more brisk. The air was redolent of feedyards; Clayton, like Carroll, was cattle country. In fact, raising cattle was about all the land was good for. The immediate area was full of extinct volcanoes, and the top soil was a thin layer that supported grass, weeds, and a few varieties of hardy trees, mostly pine of one sort or another. It was not good farming land.

Tucking his briefcase under his arm, he looked around for the jail. He saw a small building, constructed of the same brick as the courthouse, with bars on the windows and closed his eyes for a moment. That absolutely could not be the jail; that structure was old when Cain killed Abel. Blinking open his eyes he noticed a sign with an arrow directing him toward the sheriff's office, a tiny brick building equally as old as the jail.

Charles opened an old screen door and found himself in a small foyer with four offices opening off it. Crawford County's jail facility was scruffy, antiquated, and inadequate; but compared to this jail, it was clean, modern, and roomy.

"May I help you?" asked a deputy seated behind a desk in the office directly in front of the door. Slim and Hispanic, the young man peered at him through a pair of aviation glasses that obviously contained prescription lenses. Either that or he suffered from a serious thyroid disorder, because his eyes seemed almost protruberant behind the tinted glass.

Puzzled, Charles examined him. His uniform looked cleaner, newer, and better pressed than anything his own deputies wore. His black, curly hair was carefully groomed, his badge pinned dead center on his breast pocket, his smile polite and impersonal. Still, there was something familiar about him. "Yes, I want to see Sheriff Lindman."

The deputy hesitated and nervously pushed his glasses further up his nose. "What business did you wish to discuss with the sheriff?"

"I'm Charles Matthews," he said, shifting uneasily. The name sounded incomplete without the title of sheriff preceding it. "I'm Raul Trujillo's attorney."

The deputy scratched his head, and Charles again felt an elusive sense of recognition. "Well, the sheriff's real busy right now. He's in conference."

"Then I'll talk to my client."

The deputy squinted over Charles's shoulder at a closed door. "Well, I don't know about that," he said.

Charles resisted the impulse to jerk the man out of his chair and shake him like a terrier with a rat. Instead he set his briefcase on the floor and, placing both palms flat on the desk, leaned over. "In that case, son," he said in a conversational tone of voice, "I'll just drive down to Santa Fe, go to the federal court there, and file a lawsuit. When I'm finished, I'll own you, the sheriff, and *this whole damn jail!*" he finished in a roar.

The silence in the little room was so complete that the deputy's noisy swallowing seemed to echo. "I—I—" he stuttered.

"What in the hell is going on out here?"

The deputy jumped up, or tried to. Unfortunately he had failed to push his chair back first. His thighs hit the edge of the desk with predictable results. He staggered backward into his chair and tipped it over. Charles observed that the young man's boots, now occupying the space where his head had been, were highly polished.

Glancing around, Charles saw a wiry, middle-aged man in Western shirt and slacks, leaning heavily against the wall of the foyer. One hand covered his eyes, and he was shaking his head like a bull who had just run into an electrified fence.

"Get up off the floor, 'Tonio," said the man, lowering his hand and pushing himself away from the wall.

Ignoring the scrambling and scraping noises of 'Tonio, the man walked into the little office, eyes fixed on Charles. "Now, what's this about my jail?"

Charles always wondered later if his mouth had really fallen open, or if it just felt that way. Sheriff Christopher "Kit" Lindman, the legend of Northern New Mexico, the man with the Nordic name, was indisputably Hispanic from the top of his wavy blue-black hair to the bottoms of his boots. The only things he'd inherited from his father were a pair of bright blue eyes and a faint inflection on the ends of his sentences. He almost, but not quite, had a Norwegian accent.

Charles cleared his throat. "As I explained to your deputy, I'm Raul Trujillo's attorney."

"He wanted to talk to you, Sheriff, but you were busy. Then he wanted to see the prisoner, but you said not to let anyone see him without telling you first." 'Tonio had managed to climb to his feet. "Then he threatened to sue," he finished dramatically.

Lindman rolled his eyes skyward, or at least toward the ceiling. " 'Tonio, do you use your head for anything but a place to hang your hat? Where's your judgment, son? If I'm talking to the president and a murder suspect's lawyer comes visiting, particularly this murder suspect's lawyer, you interrupt. You understand? 'Cause if you don't and he sues this county for its last head of cattle, you're going to be dead. I'm going to skin you alive, tan your hide, and hang it on my office wall."

'Tonio wiggled apologetically. Were all young deputies related to puppies? Charles wondered. "President of what, Sheriff?"

This time Lindman's eyes threatened to disappear altogether as he rolled them upward. He shook his head in resignation. "Get Trujillo's file, son. And don't drop it," he added.

Lindman turned back to Charles. "The mayor's wife's cousin's boy. Took a bunch of law enforcement courses and decided he wanted to be a sheriff. He's not such a bad kid, just young. No judgment; takes everything literally. He'll be a good peace officer some day. If I live that long."

"I have a deput—er, employee like 'Tonio," said Charles, thinking of Slim. "They require a little extra guidance."

Lindman made a sound suspiciously like a snort. "And a boot applied to their behinds." He opened a file folder that a much subdued 'Tonio handed him. Silently he passed it to Charles.

Leafing through the file, Charles frowned. It contained a yellow teletype, a fingerprint card, a report from the arresting officer, and a mug shot that made Raul look like a criminal. Nothing unusual about that. What was unusual, like the dog that didn't bark in the night, was the amount of missing material.

He looked at Lindman, his eyes like obsidian and just as hard. "Where's the rest of it? The photographs of the scene of the crime, the statements from witnesses, the autopsy report?"

"I have it," answered a nasal voice. It belonged to a tall blond man with red-rimmed eyes. After smothering a gigantic sneeze in a wrinkled white handkerchief, the man blew his reddened nose with an apologetic air. "Sorry, allergy to sagebrush. And to everything else that grows around here," he added bitterly.

Tucking the handkerchief in his breast pocket, he held out his hand. "Inspector Ed Polanski, FBI."

Automatically Charles shook hands. "Charles Matthews," he said slowly, feeling another gust of uneasiness that had nothing to do with his guilt at hiding his identity. "What does the FBI have to do with Raul?"

"It wouldn't have had anything to do with your client if he'd had the common decency to commit his murder a half mile away. Or if the park superintendent hadn't demanded I be called in. The FBI usually lets the local constabulary handle this sort of thing. Unless it involves a federal employee or nationally elected official, of course. I told him that. But no; nothing will do but that I drive up here and oversee the investigation." The inspector grabbed for his handkerchief. "I'm a city boy, from Chicago. I don't like all this empty space."

Sheriff Lindman raised his voice to be heard over the truly magnificent sneezes coming from Polanski. " 'Tonio,

24

run over and pick up the prisoner, and buy the inspector some nose drops while you're out." He turned to Charles. "We keep county prisoners at the city jail. This one was condemned several years back."

Polanski blew his nose again. "The FBI doesn't enjoy getting involved in these family quarrels that end in sordid violence." He waved his arm. "Why didn't Mr. Trujillo simply dispose of his cousin in the privacy of his own home? Why defame a national monument? The secretary of the interior is going to be very unhappy about this."

Charles rubbed his stomach with a circular motion. His medication was beginning to wear off, and the allergy-ridden inspector's habit of talking around the subject of the murder wasn't helping his indigestion. "Just what in the hell are you talking about?"

Inspector Polanski folded his handkerchief and looked at the sheriff out of eyes any drunk would have been proud of. "Your client murdered his cousin, Enrique Armijo, inside the crater of Mount Capulin, which has been a national monument since August sixth, nineteen-sixteen when President Wilson set aside six hundred and eighty acres to preserve 'a striking example of recent extinct volcanoes.' Some young ranger found the body this morning, thankfully before visiting hours began. The park superintendent has developed a stutter from nervous tension. First we rope off the scene of the crime and won't let the tourists inside the crater. Then we block off the entire monument while we look for the rest of the murder weapon."

Charles was beginning to think he was Alice lost in Wonderland. The entire story had a surrealistic quality Lewis Carroll would have enjoyed. "What do you mean the 'rest of the murder weapon'? Did you lose part of it?"

Sheriff Lindman answered while Polanski was involved

in trying to prevent another sneeze. "The weapon was designed in two pieces for use with a third piece. Apparently the murderer didn't know that. When he attempted to remove the weapon, it came apart."

"What kind of weapon are you talking about?"

Inspector Polanski interrupted with an irritated look at Lindman. Evidently the inspector felt some territorial rights concerning the case. "According to Doctor Hagan from the university, it was a very primitive weapon. Of course, I wanted it sent straight to the FBI lab in Washington, but we did need to get some idea of the type of weapon rather quickly, so I consented to the New Mexico's state police lab's request for a consultation with Doctor Hagan."

Sheriff Lindman's blue eyes seem to have shards of a glacier in them. "What do you mean 'consented to'? I thought you were here purely as an advisor, but that the investigation was mine."

"Of course, of course," Polanski reassured him. "Just as long as you keep me informed so I *can* advise you. You can rely on my superior training to help you."

Lindman's mouth was pursed up as if he'd bitten into something very bitter. "I'm sure," he muttered.

"What kind of weapon are you talking about, and who is Doctor Hagan?" asked Charles ominously.

"Doctor Hagan is an archeologist and anthropologist, with a good reputation in both fields, I believe. I'm not arguing with his qualifications you understand. I'd just feel more comfortable with the FBI lab and its experts."

"You're saying New Mexico doesn't have experts worth trusting?" asked Sheriff Lindman.

Polanski wiped his forehead and drew a deep breath. "Far be it from me to insult the state of New Mexico, Sheriff Lindman. I just meant that our lab has so many more resources at its disposal with which to examine physical evidence."

"*What kind of weapon are you talking about?*" Charles roared.

Both men turned to stare at him, and the inspector drew another breath. As if the sheriff weren't being difficult enough, now he had to deal with this attorney. "An atl-atl," replied Polanski.

"A what?" asked Charles blankly.

"A spear thrower used thousands of years ago by primitive tribes. The foreshaft with the projectile point was still in the wound, but the main shaft and atl-atl were gone."

"And you found them on Mount Capulin?" asked Charles.

"No," said Lindman. "We found them in Raul Trujillo's hotel room. The shaft still had his cousin's blood on it."

5

CHARLES SAT AT Sheriff Lindman's desk waiting for
'Tonio to arrive with Raul. Too bad he couldn't tell
Lindman who he really was. He'd enjoy exchanging
information with another county sheriff; he suspected
they'd have a lot in common.

He rose when 'Tonio escorted Raul in. Raul had the
stunned, disbelieving expression of a man whose world
has suddenly and inexplicably shattered. His olive skin
had overtones of gray around the mouth and eyes. But
these were superficial changes. What worried Charles
was the sense of grief that seemed to envelop his deputy,
as if something essential were in danger of being lost.
And it is, thought Charles. Raul had a certain gentle
empathy, an ability to focus on whatever goodness a
man might possess. It was difficult to remain empathetic,
or to perceive goodness, while in jail.

"Sit down, Mr. Trujillo," he said formally, motioning
to a chair in front of the desk. "That will be all," he said
to 'Tonio, his eyes warning Raul to be silent.

"Sheriff," began Raul hesitantly as soon as the door
closed behind 'Tonio.

"Mr. Matthews, please," cautioned Charles. "I'm here
as your attorney."

Raul lowered his voice. "Does Sheriff Lindman know?"

"Does he know I'm an attorney? Of course."

Raul looked reproachfully at him, and Charles shifted
uneasily. "No," he admitted. "He doesn't know who I
am. But as a Texas sheriff, I couldn't help you. I would

have no authority to question witnesses, to examine the scene of the crime, to study Lindman's file. As an attorney, I can do all those things."

Raul studied him. "And who is sheriff of Crawford County while you're doing all these things?"

Charles took a legal pad and a pen from his briefcase. "Meenie can handle it. Right now I'm more concerned about you. I need to know some background. Why were you and your cousin staying at this hotel in"—he paused and looked at his notes—"Folsom, New Mexico?"

"Enrique is an archeologist"—he caught his error—"*was* an archeologist. He was on a dig at the old Folsom Man site."

"Why wasn't he staying at the dig?"

Raul's mouth twisted. "Enrique liked to be"—he hesitated—"comfortable."

Charles cocked an eyebrow. In his experience people who thought a lot of being comfortable tended to be self-centered. "According to the statements from the witnesses, you argued with Armijo over some land."

"Yes," Raul answered. He wiped his hand over his face, and Charles noticed its trembling. "My mother's family settled in New Mexico over two hundred and fifty years ago and acquired some land." He hesitated a second, as though recognizing that the acquisition had been without the consent of the original owners. "Not a ranch like in Texas. Not so large as that, but good land along the Rio Grande. We held it against Indian attacks and against the Anglos when they claimed New Mexico and broke up the large land grants. The land has no loyalty. It belongs to the man who can hold it. And we have held it for two hundred and fifty years. It has passed from father to son."

Raul clenched his fist until the knuckles turned white from the pressure. "But my grandfather had no sons, only daughters. So the oldest grandson inherited—my cousin, Enrique. He knew he was never to sell. It was understood; the land must stay in the family. I took part of my vacation to come to New Mexico to talk to him, to make him understand. I talked about pride and family and the land. He only cared about money, how many dollars per acre the land would bring. Friday night at dinner, in front of everyone in the hotel, he told me he had sold the land."

Raul's olive skin was shiny with sweat, and his eyes seemed to have sunk deep into his skull. He looked at Charles in hopeless desperation. "I was angry, crazy with it. I told Enrique I would kill him before I'd let him betray the family. He laughed at me and said I'd have to hurry, because the papers were to be signed the next day. The next day he was dead."

Raul's words seemed to hang in the air, and Charles felt his own desperation. Raul had the oldest motive for murder there was: money. But it was too soon to panic. Better to hear the rest of Raul's story, compare it to the witnesses' statements. Somewhere there was an inconsistency.

He consulted his notes. "After the argument, your cousin left the hotel to observe some kind of ceremony."

"The Skin People," interrupted Raul.

Charles raised an eyebrow. "What?"

"The Skin People," repeated Raul. "That's what the locals call them. They dress in animal skins that they tan themselves and live in a commune on some ranch."

"A commune! I thought that sort of thing went out of style when the hippies grew up."

"They're not hippies. They're different. They try to live like Folsom Man did ten thousand years ago. They even use stone axes to chop their wood."

"They're a cult?" asked Charles. "They worship Folsom Man?"

Raul rubbed his forehead in frustration. "No, they act

like they *are* Folsom Man, or almost. I can't tell you anything else about them. They were always at the dig, just watching and sometimes chanting. I gave some flowers I'd picked to one of the girls and the leader gave me such a look that I stayed away from all of them after that." He shivered. "I felt afraid."

Charles leaned over and grasped his shoulder. "Take it easy, Raul; you're getting a case of jailhouse nerves. Go on with your story. After your cousin left the hotel, what did you do?"

Raul slumped back in his chair. "I went for a walk, Sheriff. I do not like to argue, and to argue with family leaves a bad feeling."

"Did you meet anybody on this walk? Did anybody see you?"

"No. The hotel is just outside Folsom, and I walked in the country, not toward town. But if I'd gone the other way, it would be the same. No one would have seen me."

Charles leaned back in his chair. "Oh? And why not?"

"It's a tiny place. There isn't even a convenience store. Everyone is home with their families at night. It's peaceful," he added sadly, as if peace were something he might not experience again.

Peaceful towns where everyone stayed off the streets at night, with or without convenience stores, didn't provide good alibis, Charles thought grimly. He consulted his notes. "No one saw or heard you come back to the hotel? Why didn't the desk clerk see you?"

"There isn't a desk clerk."

Charles looked up. "What do you mean? What kind of a hotel is it?"

Raul smiled. "A very old one. It has three stories, but only the first two are used. It's more like a boarding house; there are only six rooms to rent and only five were rented. A guest takes a front-door key if he's going to be out late."

Charles shook his head. "That's great. Why couldn't you have stayed at a Holiday Inn?"

"I didn't know I was going to be suspected of murder."

"I'm sorry, Raul; I wasn't trying to be funny. I was venting my own frustration." He waved the statements. "I expected you to refute these, not support them. You threatened your cousin, you haven't got an alibi for the time of his murder, and the weapon was found in your closet. But the prosecution still has to prove that you even knew what an atl-atl was, much less how to use it. I don't think it's something you can just pick up and throw with any accuracy without practice."

Raul looked down at the desk. "There was an atl-atl-throwing contest at the hotel. I didn't win, but I hit the target every time." He shrugged his shoulders. "I seem to have a natural talent for it."

"Who did win?" demanded Charles.

Raul looked at his friend, a grim smile on his lips. "Enrique did."

"Damn!" exclaimed Charles. Motive, opportunity, weapon; Raul had it all. He glanced down at his notepad. He had drawn boxes, each one divided into smaller boxes and all as confining as the evidence.

With a vicious curse he ripped the page from his notepad, crushed it into a ball, and threw it against the wall. Damn it, the evidence was wrong. Raul did not have the kind of character to commit deliberate murder.

"And the others staying at the hotel, these people who made statements?"

Raul counted off on his fingers. "Bob and Mary James own the hotel. He's a retired mining engineer and amateur archeologist. He goes to the dig every day. Then there's Dr. Hagan. He's chairman of the archeology department at the University of New Mexico. The other guest is David Lessing. He's a graduate student and was Enrique's assistant."

"In other words, they were all involved with your cousin and the dig?"

Raul nodded. "Yes."

"Which one had a motive to murder your cousin? More to the point, which one would deliberately frame you?" Charles asked and saw the first emotion besides hopelessness on his deputy's face.

Raul straightened, then slumped back on his chair and closed his eyes. "I don't know the answer to either question, Sheriff." He opened his eyes to look at Charles. "Enrique wasn't easy to like, but I have been here less than a week. How can I know who hated him enough to kill him? And how can I be hated so much so quickly that someone would frame me?"

Charles flinched inwardly at the hurt he saw in Raul's eyes. His deputy was *muy simpatico,* a very sympathetic man toward others. That type of person found it difficult to believe anyone could hate him. "Raul," he said slowly, "could it be just random chance? You were in the right place at the right time and provided the murderer with the perfect scapegoat?"

Raul looked horrified. "That is worse than hating me!"

"What do you mean?" asked Charles.

His deputy shivered. "If someone hates me, then I understand if they hurt me. It is natural, human." He smiled. "Not a good thing, but human. To hurt me just because I am there, to hurt so coldly, that is not natural. That is a twisted soul, a *bruja,* a witch."

Charles smiled, lending his features a charm he was unaware of. "Raul," he chided, "you're being superstitious."

Raul rubbed his chin where a dark stubble was showing. "No, it's not that. There is a darkness, an evil about this one." He grabbed Charles's hand. "Don't you understand? If you come into this, you'll be in danger."

"For God's sake, Raul, do you think I'm a kid? I have a scar on my back less than six months old because I was a threat to a murderer. I know murderers are dangerous."

"Did you know that sometimes the rattlesnake strikes without giving warning?"

"No, I didn't, but don't worry, I'll carry a snakebite kit."

"It's not a joke, Sheriff."

"I know it," said Charles impatiently. "But I'm not in the mood for any Western metaphors. I'm going after the bastard that deliberately set you up, and I don't think he's the Devil in disguise. Besides, I don't always give any warning before I strike either."

He stood up. "You'll be formally charged tomorrow, and I'll get bail set. Will you be all right in here for one night?"

Raul's smile was humorless. "It's only bad when they close the door." He shuddered. "That's the most final sound in the world, Sheriff, because you know it can only be opened from the outside."

Charles squeezed Raul's shoulder, then walked to the door and called 'Tonio. He turned his back and stared out the window at the old jail. He flinched when he heard the handcuffs snap into place on Raul's wrists and continued looking at the window long after the door closed behind 'Tonio and his prisoner.

6

SHERIFF LINDMAN WAS waiting for him when he finally opened the door and walked into the foyer. "Mr. Matthews," he said, grasping Charles's arm. "Step back into my office. If you don't mind," he added.

Charles shrugged. "No, I don't mind. I need to talk to you anyway. There's the matter of formal charges. And bail, of course."

"Of course," agreed Lindman politely. "In here, please." Closing the door behind them, he gestured toward a chair. "Set down."

Charles sat down and surveyed Lindman's office as if he hadn't already seen it once. Lindman's desk looked to be as old as his own, the filing cabinet as battered, and the chairs just as uncomfortable. The smell was the same—disinfectant, stale cigarette smoke, human perspiration—only fainter.

A sneeze drew his attention to the room's third occupant. Inspector Polanski nodded at Charles. "Sagebrush. It's all this damn sagebrush around here. Whole state's covered with the stuff. If they could figure out a use for it, New Mexico would be the richest state in the union."

Lindman sat down behind his desk and picked up a pencil. He rolled it between his fingers like a piece of clay and looked at Charles. He wore a massive silver ring, set with turquoise, on his right hand, and the pencil clicked against it with monotonous regularity.

"Tell me," Lindman asked quietly, each word emphasized with a roll of the pencil and its accompanying click. "What the hell are you up to, *Sheriff Matthews*?"

He snapped the pencil in two and stood up. "You think I'm a fool? We get the Amarillo paper in Clayton, we watch television here. You're famous, you and Crawford County. All that business last summer with the murders and that gold cross and you getting shot. Did you think we didn't hear about it? Did you think I didn't see you on network TV? You're supposed to be a real hero, an old-fashioned sheriff, somebody the rest of us peace officers can be proud of."

He circled around the desk and, grabbing the arms of Charles's chair, leaned over him. "Just what the hell are you doing sneaking around Union County like a damn coyote looking over a herd of spring calves?"

Charles stared into Lindman's cold blue eyes so close to his own and felt like a teenager caught trying to seduce the preacher's daughter in the choir loft on Sunday morning. There was that same feeling of having done something disgraceful, of having sullied something pure. But, damn it, he hadn't.

His hands tightened into fists. "I left my badge in Texas. I'm an attorney now."

Lindman let go of the chair and straightened up. "You don't stop being a sheriff just because you left your badge on your dresser this morning. What did you have in mind? Were you gonna come up here and show us New Mexicans how it's done? You planning on tracking down a murderer and bringing in his scalp?"

Charles rose and kicked his chair out of the way. "Yes, damn it, I will if that's what it takes."

"Then you better go lift your deputy's hair, 'cause he's guilty as sin. We got the evidence to prove it."

"I don't care if you found him crouching over the body with blood on his hands. Raul is incapable of murder."

"Just how the hell do you figure that?"

Charles took a deep breath. "Because he doesn't have the character to murder someone, anyone, especially a member of his own family."

Polanski interrupted. "I think you lack a certain objectivity, Sheriff Matthews. Statistically, a majority of murders are committed by family members. I don't have the exact figures, but the FBI has done a great deal of work on psychological profiles of murderers and—"

"Raul isn't a murderer, damn it! So you can take your psychological profiles and—"

"Silencio!" shouted Lindman, and Charles grinned in spite of his frustration. Lindman's Norwegian accent was even more noticeable when he spoke Spanish.

Lindman's sharp gaze shifted between Charles and Polanski until satisfied there wouldn't be blood spilled on his waxed tile floor. He circled around his desk and sat down. "Now, Sheriff, I want to hear more about Mr. Trujillo's character."

"Sheriff Lindman," interrupted the inspector. "I've been satisfied to allow you to direct this investigation, but this discussion is completely counterproductive. We found the murder weapon in Mr. Trujillo's hotel room where he'd obviously hidden it. The bureau will object most strenuously to any delay—"

Lindman slammed his hand on his desk. His turquoise ring made a satisfactory cracking sound on its surface. "Inspector Polanski, I don't give a dried cow patty what the FBI says. Now you just sit there nice and quiet while I listen to what Sheriff Matthews has to say, or I'll gag you with your own handkerchief and tie you to the nearest pinyon tree."

The inspector looked horrified. "I'm allergic to pinyon."

Lindman rolled his eyes toward the ceiling for a second, then nodded at Charles. "Go on, Sheriff."

Charles ran his fingers through his hair as he gathered his thoughts. He wished he'd listened to Meenie. Sheriff Lindman was definitely not a man to cross. He felt sweat bead on his forehead as a series of burning spasms rippled through his belly. God, this wasn't the time to be distracted by pain. He was about to have to make a persuasive argument, and he had not a shred of evidence to present in Raul's favor.

"Raul has been my deputy for almost three years. But he was a deputy for my predecessor for ten years before that. Thirteen years of wearing a badge, of carrying a gun."

Charles rose and leaned over Lindman's desk. A second of losing his temper, and a man could die. "But in those thirteen years Raul has never used his gun except in the line of duty. He's never killed anyone."

Lindman touched his badge thoughtfully. "I've been a lawman most of my life, and I've never met the deputy who didn't lose his temper every now and then."

Charles straightened and stuck his hands in his pockets. "Yes," he admitted. "But how many have you known who could commit murder?"

"Are you trying to tell me your deputy isn't capable of killing a man at all?" asked Lindman softly.

"No," Charles said. "Only that he wouldn't follow a man several miles and coldly stab him."

Polanski sniffed. "He wasn't stabbed precisely, and you keep forgetting the evidence. Examination of the physical evidence proves that—"

"Damn little," interrupted Lindman. He glared at the inspector. "Hell, it's the man that kills, not the damn spear point. It just lies there until someone picks it up, ties it on the end of a stick, and throws it at somebody."

Polanski's red-streaked eyes widened as much as their swollen state allowed. "Surely you're not intending to release Mr. Trujillo. Because if you are, I will be forced to take charge of the case."

Charles whirled around toward the FBI agent, his hands coming out of his pockets and balling into fists when Lindman forestalled him. "Sit down, Sheriff Matthews," roared Lindman.

He folded his hands again and somberly looked at Polanski. "Inspector, I have a lot of respect for the bureau. Most of the time. Even your critics, when they were busy opening Mr. Hoover's closets after his death and looking for all the skeletons, never said too much bad about the bureau itself. Nobody's ever accused you men of taking bribes, or lying, or sending a man to prison without proper evidence."

Polanski pushed his chest out. "Thank you, Sheriff Lindman."

Lindman rubbed his jaw. "But the bureau's used to seeing the big picture. And that's good. Country's got to have that. You chase bank robbers and kidnappers and spies. But you don't arrest drunks on Saturday night. You don't have to break up a family fight. Domestic violence, it's called, and it accounts for about thirty per cent or more of the police calls made every week. You don't see the kids abused by parents too dumb or too mean or too sick to know any better. You don't generally investigate murder. What I'm saying is that in your job you don't have to figure out people the way Sheriff Matthews and I do."

Polanski sighed and carefully blew his nose. "I think I've just been told to mind my own business. You realize, of course, that I have the authority to take over the investigation." He glanced at Charles and swallowed hastily. He wished he hadn't added that last remark.

Lindman nodded. "I know it. And I'm asking you not to do it. You see, I have a personal interest in this case. I don't like crooked lawmen. In .fact, the only people I hate worse are the ones who try to frame honest deputies for murder."

Charles expelled a breath. "Thank you, Sheriff."

Lindman held up a hand. "Not so fast, Matthews. I'm gonna be real fair about this. I'm willing to be convinced that your deputy is pure as the driven snow. I'm just as willing to be convinced that he's a low-down murdering varmint. But what I'm not willing to do is have you running all over Union County like some West Texas Perry Mason."

He reached in a desk drawer and pulled out a deputy's badge. "You were talking about oaths, Sheriff, like you believed in them. I hope so, because any man who works with me has to swear an oath to uphold the laws of this county and of this state." He held out his hand toward Charles, the badge lying in his palm. "Put it on, Matthews. If you're planning on investigating this murder, you're gonna do it as my deputy."

Charles stared at the piece of metal. He couldn't put it on. He couldn't put duty between himself and Raul. As an attorney he was safe. His first loyalty would be to his client. But as a deputy his first loyalty would be to the truth. He squeezed his eyes shut. And if the truth turned out to be that Raul was guilty, his own oath would force him to be Raul's accuser.

"No," he whispered, looking at Lindman from tortured eyes. "I can't."

Never taking his eyes from Charles's, Lindman laid the badge in the middle of his desk. "Are you afraid he's guilty?"

Charles felt the question send another burning spasm through him. "And if he is?" he asked in a hoarse voice.

Lindman's eyes lost their focus as he gazed at the opposite wall. "You'll feel like a horse kicked you in the belly."

7

THE FARTHER FROM Clayton Charles drove, the more he sensed Northern New Mexico had a wilder feel than the Texas Panhandle. It might be the dozens of extinct volcanoes, dominated by the sharp profile of Mount Capulin, or the purple smudges on the horizon that marked the Sangre de Cristo Mountains. Or it might be the idea of the contradictions to be found in the state: Los Alamos and the remains of cliff dwellings, modern Albuquerque and ancient Taos Pueblo. Whatever it was, it was real; as real as Mount Capulin, as real as the old building that loomed ahead.

Charles stopped in front of the hotel and rubbed the back of his neck. The new scar across his shoulder blades felt raw and tender. Gingerly he reached over his shoulder and touched it. He'd been shot while investigating what the press had called the Branding Iron Murders, and he could do without ever being shot again. Of course it didn't help that he'd gotten the wound infected when he'd climbed back on a horse and rejoined the manhunt. He shuddered. Riding a horse was something else he could do without.

Hoping for a hot bath to soak away his stiffness from the tension of the interminable day, he got out of the car and took his first good look at the hotel. The place didn't look as if it had indoor plumbing, much less private bathrooms. It was a narrow, three-story building so old the mortar between the bricks seemed to be crumbling. It stood alone on the side of asphalt highway, flanked by two huge cottonwood trees and the top of another visible behind it. A roofed veranda, or porch, jutted out across the front of the building. Wide, shallow steps led up to it. Charles felt a hysterical laugh building up inside when he realized the steps were wood. My God, add a hitching post and a watering trough, and the whole thing could have been lifted out of the nineteenth century. He felt as if he were caught in a time warp. Or had inadvertently wandered onto a movie set.

Reaching into the back seat he lifted out a suitcase and locked the car. Against whom he couldn't imagine. He hadn't seen anyone since leaving Clayton. He hadn't even passed any cars. The landscape looked and felt devoid of life.

Straightening, he looked south toward Mount Capulin. The extinct volcano loomed black in the gathering twilight. Its stark silhouette looked like a worn, crumbling tombstone erected eons ago over the grave of some long-dead giant. *Dead or merely sleeping,* he wondered. Wasn't there a folktale in Hawaii about a mountain that was really a sleeping giant? And didn't the folktale end with a warning never to wake him lest he bring destruction and desolation to the island?

As the twilight faded into night, Capulin seemed larger and nearer, and Charles felt suspended in some gloomy, surrealistic world. Giving in to the hysteria that had been building up, he leaned against the car and laughed until the utter stillness around him seemed to echo with the sound. To his own ears he sounded maniacal, and he choked back the sound, shuddering with the effort. Picking up the suitcase he'd dropped, he walked toward the hotel. First it was Raul with his talk of devils, then his own fanciful thoughts of sleeping giants. Next he'd be seeing ghosts.

A sharp object poked him in the back, and he dropped his suitcase.

42

"Just walk straight up those steps and into the hotel so I can get a look at you in the light." The object prodded him again. "Go on, walk," repeated the voice.

Charles walked, his heartbeat slowing down. Unless ghosts spoke in a flat Midwestern accent and smelled of cigars, whoever was behind him was at least corporeal. "No need to threaten me," he said dryly. "I was planning on renting a room anyway."

The voice chuckled. "Were you now? Well, let's see if you meet our specifications as a guest. Open the door and meet the selection committee."

The door was actually two doors, solid wood with etched glass panels in the top half of each. *Authentic,* thought Charles, *but not very practical. A thief with a sharp glasscutter could have those doors open in about thirty seconds. A thief might be unwise to try it,* he thought as he opened the doors to face a short, wiry woman with graying blond hair neatly braided in a coronet on top of her head. She held a rifle pointed at his belly, and her stance couldn't have been more professional if she'd been a twenty-year veteran in the army.

He cleared his throat. "You must be the selection committee," he said, removing his Stetson.

"He doesn't appear to be crazy," said the already familiar voice. "And I didn't smell liquor on him." A tall, thin man, with a fringe of sandy hair circling his head, stepped around Charles to join the woman. He held a very lethal-looking spear.

Charles slapped his hat back on his head. "I'm not drunk, and if anyone's crazy, it's certainly not me. If you're planning on shooting me, or stabbing me with that ridiculous spear, do it. Otherwise, I'll get back in my car and find a hotel where all they care about is whether my credit card is current. I'm hungry, tired, and well on my way to being damn mad." His chin jutted out belligerently. "What's it going to be?" he demanded.

"Well said, young man, well said," bellowed a gravelly voice from somewhere behind Charles. "I'd like to know myself. Make up your mind, Bob. Are you going to skewer him or just tell Mary to shoot him? If it's the latter, I won't bother closing the door. Wouldn't want a bullet hole in that lovely old wood."

Charles started to turn around, but a large hand grasping his shoulder from behind prevented it. "Stand still, young man." The voice had modulated to a loud roar. "Don't want to make any sudden moves. Bob might have an itchy spear hand."

Bob rested the shaft of his spear on the floor. He wiped his hand over the top of his bald head and looked embarrassed. "Now Doctor Hagan, we're kind of isolated," he began.

"So you welcome all your guests with a gun. Pardon me, spear. Wouldn't a No Vacancy sign be easier?" asked Charles sarcastically, and he heard a chuckle near the vicinity of his left ear.

"One of our guests was murdered by another guest," said the woman, her rifle still pointing at Charles. "We have a right to be suspicious of strangers who stare at the moon and laugh instead of coming inside and registering."

Charles flushed. "I wasn't staring at the moon; I was looking at Mount Capulin and imagining, well, imagining something ridiculous. I was laughing at myself."

Bob leaned his spear against the wall behind him, and looked at Charles as if he had just met a soul brother. "I know what you mean. Capulin does that to some people. You look at it, especially at night, and it seems alive. Sometimes I think I can see steam rising from its crater, and I can feel the earth shaking underneath my feet. Always quakes before an eruption, you know," he said vaguely, glancing at Charles with eyes that seemed to be looking inward, or maybe backward through time.

44

"No, I didn't," said Charles dryly, wondering if the man in front of him was crazy, or merely eccentric.

The man blinked as if coming out of a daze. He stepped toward Charles and held out his hand. "I'm Bob James, and the lady with the gun is my wife, Mary."

Mary lowered the rifle and sighed with exasperation. "I swear, Bob James, you'd rent a room to Jack the Ripper if he'd showed any interest in your old relics."

"Capulin isn't a relic," said her husband mildly. "It's a monument."

"Same thing," she muttered, gesturing at Charles. "Come sign the register. I'll never have any peace if I turn you away. Besides, you couldn't be any crazier than my husband."

"Mrs. James believes that anyone interested in grubbing about in search of old bits and pieces of stone or wood left by primitive man must be crazy," said the deep, gravelly voice as its owner stepped around Charles to face him. "Of course Capulin isn't man-made, but you must admit that a volcano, even an extinct one, is primitive." He held out a hand that would have covered a small dinner plate. "I'm Doctor Hagan."

Doctor William Alfred Hagan gave true meaning to the word "stocky." Half a head shorter than Charles's six foot three, he looked as if he had been constructed of a child's wooden blocks. His body was thick and square, his barrel-chested torso resting on broad buttocks, with only a slim leather belt to delineate where one section ended and the next began. His legs and arms were massive columns joined to this torso, while his large, square head topped a neck the size of which any football player would envy. Faded blue eyes, pure white hair, and a certain transparency of skin led Charles to estimate him to be in his sixties. Not that it mattered. A man like Doctor Hagan didn't age; he weathered.

Uncomfortably aware he'd been staring, Charles hastily shook the doctor's hand. "Charles Matthews," he said, his voice trailing off as he noticed the doctor's tie for the first time. It was an abominable creation of bright yellow sunflowers intertwined with green leaves against a dark brown background. It added to Charles's feeling that he was shaking hands with a stone monolith, one with flowers clinging tenaciously to its surface.

Doctor Hagan chuckled at Charles's reaction. "I'm an archeologist. And occasionally an anthropologist. When a man is born looking like one of the statues on Easter Island, it seems the natural choice of professions. But what about you, young man? What brings you to Folsom Hotel? If you don't mind my saying so, you look like you'd be more at home at the Hyatt Regency," he said, eyeing Charles's expensive sport coat.

Charles shrugged off the comment. He'd been told often enough in the Panhandle that he looked out of place. Evidently the same thing held true in Northern New Mexico. What he couldn't shrug off was the doctor's question. He'd hoped to have time to observe everyone at the hotel, form some impression of them before revealing himself.

"I'm Raul Trujillo's attorney." He wondered briefly if he'd be escorted back to his car by spear point.

Other than surprise, he could detect no reaction from the three. Walking over to small hotel desk just to the right of a stair case, Mary James flipped open a thick old book with yellowing pages and held out a pen to Charles. "You should have said so to start with. I don't think I've heard of too many lawyers murdering people in their beds; they just defend the folks who do."

"Raul is *not* a murderer," said Charles through clenched teeth. Obviously Mary James wasn't a strong believer in the concept of innocent until proven guilty.

She smiled sympathetically. "Of course he is," she said firmly. "No one else had a reason to kill Enrique."

"And if you believe that, Mr. Attorney, I have a map to the Lost Dutchman, the West's most famous vanished gold mine. It's guaranteed authentic, and it's all yours. For a price, of course." The speaker, a new arrival, dropped a rucksack on the floor and put his hands on his hips, a mocking smile on his lips.

Bob James cleared his throat. "This is David Lessing. He is, uh, was Doctor Armijo's graduate assistant."

Charles's first thought was that graduate assistants looked younger these days; his second, that if Dr. Hagan looked like an Easter Island statue, then David Lessing could have served as a model for a sculpture of a Roman god. He had the requisite noble brow; well-formed eyebrows; large, liquid eyes; black hair that fell in loose curls over his sweatband; and an aquiline nose. He'd look good in a toga, better than in the Levi's and ragged sweat shirt he wore.

"And another crazy person," said Mary James suddenly. "But this one's determined to make trouble. He's accusing one of *us* of murder."

Bob James nervously pulled a cigar out of his breast pocket and stuck it in his mouth, wrapping and all. "Now, hon, David just meant Enrique wasn't a likable person."

His wife glared at him in exasperation. "Oh, for goodness sake, Bob; unwrap that cigar." She turned to David. "And you just hush, young man. Go wash your hands and come into the kitchen. I've kept a plate from supper warm for you."

David jerked off the sweat band and ran his fingers through his hair. "I'm not accusing anyone, and I don't want any supper. I'm just saying that Mr. Attorney doesn't act like a hick-town lawyer. I missed seeing just how Bob got the drop on him, but I've been outside listening and watching the last few minutes, and I've concluded we'd better revise our game plan. Anyone who can stay so calm while looking down Mary's rifle is too smart to buy our story that everyone loved Armijo except his cousin. So defend your positions, team; the opponents' star player just came into the game."

Charles clenched his teeth with anger at the younger man's words. "This isn't a game. No one is counting points on a scoreboard, and you don't shake hands with your opponents and walk off to the locker room. This is murder, and the loser dies."

David's cheeks flushed dull red under his tan. "It was just a figure of speech."

"Meaning what?" demanded Charles.

David licked his lips. "Meaning you're going to jump on every word we say and twist it into something else, so we all might as well admit that Armijo didn't exactly inspire brotherly love in our hearts. That guy knew just where to hit to give you a bruise."

"Are you admitting that all of you in this room had a motive?" asked Charles, refusing to believe what he was hearing.

"No! But if you'd caught us lying about not liking Armijo, then you wouldn't believe us about anything else. It just seemed a stupid chance to take. We could dislike Armijo and still not murder him." He shrugged his shoulders. "I'll graduate next spring, so I could ignore his comments about my being incompetent for one more semester."

Mary James nodded. "And I wouldn't murder a man because he made remarks about my cooking." She gestured at her husband. "If Bob killed everybody he argued with about his precious Folsom Man, there wouldn't be an archeologist left alive."

Charles turned to Dr. Hagan. "What about you? Aren't you going to deny hating Armijo enough to kill him?"

"I don't believe in murder," said Dr. Hagan in a voice like the rumble of approaching thunder.

"I don't believe in it either," said Charles grimly. "And there's something else I don't believe in, and that's witnesses who volunteer self-incriminating answers to questions I haven't even asked. Why did you tell me all that, David?" he asked, stepping closer to the younger man. "Was it to impress me with how honest you were? Or was it to mislead me, to keep me from asking other questions? About your alibi, for instance? It's no good, you know. You were asleep in your room. Alone. You didn't hear anything; you didn't see anyone. But no one heard or saw you."

David backed up a step. "I didn't kill Armijo," he whispered, his eyes flickering away from Charles's direct gaze.

"I didn't say you did," said Charles. "I said your alibi isn't believable." He glanced at the other three. "None of your alibis are. You all went to your rooms immediately after Raul went on his walk, and no one left them the rest of the night. *And no one heard a single sound.* Not a floorboard creaking, not a door closing, not even a toilet flushing. You all claim to have slept like the dead in a hotel as quiet as a tomb."

"You've got a lot of gall, young man, calling us liars when that client of yours doesn't have an alibi that'll hold water any better than a sieve." Mary James folded her arms across her chest and stared at Charles as if daring him to dispute her.

"But that's just the point, isn't it, Mr. Attorney? Our alibis aren't any better than Raul's," said David. He looked at Charles, a gray undertone to his tan, as though the blood had drained from his face. "If that atl-atl hadn't been found in Raul's closet, he wouldn't be in jail."

"But they did find it there," interrupted Bob James. "It doesn't make any difference if our alibis are any good or not. You can't argue away that atl-atl, Mr. Matthews."

Charles shook his head. "You're wrong. I can account for it very easily. If Raul is innocent, then someone else hid that atl-atl in his room. Someone else is the murderer."

Dr. Hagan was the first to break the silence. He peered at Charles, and the effect was like seeing a great stone idol come to life. "You said *if*, young man. Do you have some doubts about your client's innocence?"

"Raul is my friend as well as my client."

"And has a friend never lied to you?" asked Dr. Hagan, his deep voice strangely quiet.

Charles felt for a moment that he might faint. *Yes*, he wanted to scream. *A friend lied to me; a friend murdered twice and attempted murder twice more because I didn't believe he would lie. Damn you, L.D. Lassiter*, he thought bitterly; *damn you for making me doubt a friend.*

"Raul isn't lying," he replied and hoped it was true.

8

LATER, AS CHARLES stood in the small bedroom he'd been given, he decided he hadn't been completely wrong about the plumbing. While it was indoors, it had to have been installed while Victoria was still queen. Certainly the furnishings in this particular bedroom were at least that old. From the marble-topped table by the massive old bed to the oak wash stand with porcelain pitcher and bowl that stood against the opposite wall, to the clothes press in one corner, the whole room belonged in a museum.

He lay back on the bed and discovered that his feet rested flat against the footboard, and then only if he bent his knees. He twisted over on his side and heard an ominous creaking that sounded suspiciously like the rigging of an old sailing ship in a strong gale.

"It couldn't be," he muttered as he rolled off the bed and heaved the mattress up. It was. The Folsom Hotel didn't run to innerspring mattresses; it furnished its guests with rope beds instead. Charles sincerely hoped a family of mice with a taste for hemp didn't take up residence during his stay.

Kneeling, he opened his suitcase and took out his computerized chess set. He'd found that playing against a computer served two purposes: it was challenging and the time spent waiting for the computer to analyze his move and make a response allowed him a period of relaxed contemplation. God knew he needed it. He'd deliberately provoked four witnesses, and their reactions had been unexpected, to say the least. For instance, not a single one had denied lying. Even more revealing was the fact that no one had seemed surprised by his accusations, least of all David Lessing. David Lessing seemed to welcome disbelief, and that was the most interesting fact of all.

Lifting the plastic lid to the small chess set, he frowned. The placement of chess pieces looked different. He looked at the tiny display screen where the computer had printed its move and glanced back at the board. The space to which the computer directed its knight's next move was already filled.

Closing the lid, he placed the chess set to one side and examined his suitcase minutely. White half-moons formed at the corners of his clenched lips as he rose and picked his billfold off the marble-topped table. Opening it, he checked first the several slots that held his credit cards, then his cash. Satisfied, he sat down on the bed and leaned back against the headboard. *Relax,* he thought; *don't let your anger control you.*

"Damn it!" he whispered aloud as his eyes snapped open. He didn't have time to relax, and he certainly was in no mood to play psychological games with himself in order to control his temper. While he'd been soaking in the Victorian bathtub down the hall, somebody had cleverly and carefully searched his room. But not carefully enough. Whoever it was had inadvertently opened the chess set and disturbed the pieces. There was no other explanation. The set had been designed to be portable. Once the lid was closed, the pieces were held securely in place. Like most serious players, he automatically memorized the chess board with each play. He could recall the position of each piece without ever looking at the board.

He glanced at his suitcase, then at his billfold. He had his own eccentric way of packing, his own peculiar way of filing credit cards. He always tucked his rolled up socks in the four corners of his suitcase; he always filed his credit cards in alphabetical order. His socks had been moved, and his MasterCard and Visa had been switched. Someone in the hotel now knew that not only was he a Texas sheriff, so identified by a card in his billfold, but also knew he had a Union County deputy's badge tucked carelessly behind his cash. An idiot might fail to deduce that Sheriff Lindman must have extended professional courtesy and deputized him, but none of the hotel residents had struck him as being idiots.

Since he obviously had no aptitude for undercover work, he might as well start acting like a sheriff. *Or deputy*, he thought wryly as he pulled on slacks and slipped a credit card and a nail file into his pocket. Silently he opened his door. The hall was dark and quiet, and no lights shone under the doors of the other rooms. Keeping close to the wall to avoid creaking floorboards, he padded barefoot down the hall to the locked door of Enrique Armijo's room.

He had the door open in less than a minute, using the nail file, more time than it would have taken the burglar he'd prosecuted in Dallas and who had taught him how, but not too bad considering his amateur status. Closing the door quietly behind him, he flicked on the light and observed that someone had gotten there first. Papers littered the floor, and clothes were scattered about. He heard the creaking sound behind him a split second before something struck him on the head. His last thought was that he had no aptitude as a burglar either.

His first conscious thought was that for once his head hurt worse than his stomach. Cautiously he opened one eye and found himself looking into the faded blue ones of Dr. Hagan.

"Lie still, Mr. Matthews, until I check your pupils.

You've got quite a knot on your head. Chance of a concussion you know," said Hagan as he forcibly held open one eyelid, then the other, and peered suspiciously into two very black, very angry eyes. "How many fingers do you see?"

"Four," answered Charles, slapping away the doctor's hands. "I don't have a concussion. I've had one before, and I know how it feels. Besides," he added indignantly, "you're not a doctor."

Hagan looked offended. "I'll admit I'm more used to looking at a skull's empty eye sockets, but I do know something about head injuries. Most archeologists and anthropologists do. I know more about the skeletal structure than many physicians, and I can tell you you're lucky to have such a thick skull. You might have been killed, young man," he said, wagging a thick finger in Charles's face.

"Killed, Doctor? Murdered, perhaps?" asked Charles softly. Struggling up, Charles clutched the bed post and closed his eyes against the dizziness that sent the room spinning and blurred the faces of the crowd standing around the room. "Who hit me?"

Mary James looked indignant. "Certainly no one in this hotel."

"You can hardly be certain of that, can you? But I'll let the question go for a moment and ask another. Who found me?"

A gigantic sneeze from the vicinity of the doorway all but drowned out his question. "It's all the dust in this old building. Terrible on the allergies." Inspector Polanski's nasal voice was unmistakable.

"For God's sake, use some of that nose spray." The Norwegian accent was also unmistakable.

Charles peered toward the doorway and wondered if it was too late to plead concussion. For the second time he wished he'd taken Meenie's advice and not crossed

Sheriff Kit Lindman. "What are you doing here?" he asked weakly.

Lindman looked red-eyed and angry. "I'm here because somebody woke me up to tell me that the sheriff had been assaulted."

"Sheriff?" asked Dr. Hagan, one eyebrow climbing up his broad forehead.

Charles shrugged his shoulders. One person already knew his identity; there didn't seem to be any reason to continue the pretense. "I'm Sheriff Charles Matthews from Crawford County, Texas. Raul is my deputy."

Bob James, looking like a barber pole in red-striped pajamas, blinked in confusion. "I thought you were a lawyer."

"I'm that, too," Charles replied, his gaze shifting from the hotel owner to his wife, both of whom were staring at him. Dr. Hagan looked attentive, as if he'd just heard a particularly interesting line in a play. David Lessing, leaning against the clothes press in the corner, stared at the toes of his tennis shoes.

"Now that everybody knows everybody else, let's find out what happened," said Lindman. He turned his head and raised his voice to a mild bellow. " 'Tonio! Get in here!"

The young deputy popped through the door like a jack in the box, and snapped a quick salute. Unfortunately he had underestimated his distance from the FBI agent, and his elbow hit Polanski in the mouth.

The agent staggered back against the washstand and sent the china washbowl spinning. In what Charles thought was an astonishing athletic feat, 'Tonio dived sideways and caught the bowl before it hit the floor. His head caught the edge of the washstand at the same time, and he landed full length on the floor, temporarily stunned. The bowl dropped from his nerveless hands, hit the floor, cracked, and gracefully separated into two halves.

"That was an antique!" cried Mary James.

Lindman stood motionless for a few seconds, then took a step to the bed. Sinking down, he muttered a few words in Norwegian. *Amazing how profanity is unmistakable in any language,* Charles thought.

Lindman wiped his face with his hand and looked at Polanski. The agent's upper lip was rapidly swelling inside out. "I think he knocked a tooth loose," the inspector mumbled as he gingerly touched his bottom row of teeth with one finger.

Lindman's face wore an expression of infinite patience. "I know a good dentist. In the meantime, do you think you could take notes until 'Tonio, uh, wakes up? I want to find what happened out here before we have any more walking wounded."

Polanski wiped the blood from his lip, sneezed twice, blew his nose, and then pulled a notebook from his jacket pocket. "I can handle the interrogation," he said, his voice slurred.

"Can't understand a damn word you're saying," said Lindman bluntly. "Just write, and we'll let Matthews do the questioning since he's the one that got his hair parted."

Charles took a deep breath to calm his stomach and wished he'd remembered his pills. "Who found me?" he asked again.

"I did," said Mary. "I was in the kitchen baking some pies for tomorrow. I do most of my baking at night. No one to bother me then. It's cooler, too, and with no air conditioning I don't like to heat up the place in the daytime."

Considering that it was the last of October and the outside temperature was less than forty degrees, Charles thought the place could stand a little heat. He'd been regretting not bringing his thermal underwear. "So you don't know how long I'd been unconscious when you found me?"

"Maybe five minutes. I'm not really sure. I heard this heavy thud upstairs—Armijo's room is right over the kitchen—but the heater came on about the same time. The old furnace makes thumping noises most of the time, so I didn't think much about it. A minute or so later I heard another noise. Well, that was enough for me. I grabbed my broom and pounded on the ceiling. Then I wiped my hands and went up. Dr. Hagan came out of his room about the time I got to the top of the stairs and wanted to know what all the commotion was. He came with me, and we forced open the door. You were all sprawled out in front of it like a door stop. Dr. Hagan and I looked you over, and he said it was safe to move you. I woke up Bob, and he helped Dr. Hagan carry you in here."

Charles looked over Mary James's shoulder at David Lessing. He noticed the young man was still dressed in his Levi's and sweat shirt. "Were you sleeping, too?"

"No. He came in as I was starting for the stairs," said Mary.

"You saw him open the door while you were on the staircase?"

She hesitated a second. "I was coming through the dining room and heard the door open. I said, 'Who's there?' and he said, 'It's David.' I told him to come upstairs with me."

Charles looked at the young assistant. "Were you coming in, or were you about to go out?" he asked.

The young man hunched his shoulders in an instinctively defensive gesture. "I was coming in."

"Where had you been?"

David shoved his hands in his back pockets. "I was out walking."

"Where did you go? Did anybody see you?"

His eyes flickered away from Charles's, then back again. "No," he said defiantly.

"So you could just as easily been in Armijo's room assaulting me with—" he turned to Dr. Hagan. "What hit me?"

"You were hit with a rabbit stick—quite a well-preserved one, too," replied the archeologist.

"A what?" demanded Charles.

"A grooved club," interrupted Bob James. "The early Basket Makers in New Mexico, Colorado, Utah, and Arizona used them. The Pueblo Indians today still use them for communal rabbit hunts. They're made of oak or mesquite, twenty to forty inches long, one to two inches wide, and a little more than a half inch thick. The one that hit you was twenty inches long and made of mesquite. It was mine, and I sure wish people would stop stealing my artifacts."

"What do you think *you're* doing besides stealing?" asked Dr. Hagan, his booming voice causing Charles to flinch. "You should have left all those artifacts you've found *in situ* until they could have been studied by archeologists, instead of mounting them like damn animal heads."

"They were studied," replied Bob James heatedly. "I made drawings and graphs and took pictures and wrote up my findings. It's not my fault no one will publish my research papers just because I don't have a Ph.D. after my name. You're afraid, all of you ivory-tower professors, you're afraid an amateur has made the discovery of the century."

Dr. Hagan drew himself up to his full height until he looked like nothing so much as a tank preparing to roll over a hedgerow. "Now just a minute. Any scientific journal would be glad to publish your work. You'd be in demand as a speaker. You might even end up on the staff of a university. But you have to present some kind of evidence to back up your wild theories—"

A thread of spittle appeared at the corner of Bob James's mouth, and Charles revised his first impression of the hotel owner as an ineffectual, mild tempered little man. "Wild theories! Damn you academics! You wouldn't recognize a real find if you tripped over it. I tell you, Folsom Man had the atl-atl!"

"Prove it!"

"Disprove it!" shouted Bob James.

"Shut up!" roared Charles. Two startled faces turned to look at him. Polanski flinched, and Lindman merely raised one eyebrow. "I personally don't care if Folsom Man had the Colt .45 revolver. All I care about is who hit me and why."

"Sheriff?" said a hesitant voice from the doorway.

Charles felt as if he'd been hit again, this time in the belly. "Raul, damn it, what are you doing here?"

9

"THERE'S YOUR MAN," cried Mary James triumphantly. "Let a criminal out of jail, and he goes right back to being a criminal."

Charles saw his deputy flinch. Raul had been humiliated enough without having to submit to being called names.

The face he turned toward Mary James must have looked deadly because she took a step closer to her husband. More important, she thought better of saying anything else. "Thank you," Charles said, his voice no less deadly than his expression.

"Took your time getting here, didn't you?" asked Sheriff Lindman.

"I told you not to recommend bail," mumbled Polanski. "Then to talk the bail bondsman into taking title to Trujillo's car was totally irresponsible."

Lindman ignored him, his blue eyes like frozen chips of ice as he looked at Raul. "Where have you been since I let you out jail?"

"I hitchhiked as far as Capulin Village, then walked the rest of the way," replied Raul.

"Studies show that a small but not insignificant percentage of crimes are committed by suspects out on bail," continued Polanski.

"Damn it, Raul; stop taking walks by yourself," snapped Charles.

"The judge has some discretion in whether or not to grant bail in homicide cases." Polanski's swollen mouth had caused him to develop a distinct lisp.

Lindman still ignored him, but Charles noticed the sheriff's face was flushed. "You walked out of the courtroom at seven o'clock. It's now after midnight. Don't tell me it took over five hours to get here from Clayton."

"We could have easily persuaded the judge the suspect presented a danger to society."

Lindman's face was slowly becoming the color of day-old liver. He swung his head toward Polanski. "I know one member of society who's in danger"—he rose from the bed and took a step toward the inspector—"but not from the suspect."

A loud groan accompanied by spasmodic movements of arms and legs distracted Lindman, and Charles expelled a breath he wasn't aware he'd been holding. Inept deputies served a purpose: they prevented their bosses from committing felonious assault on the persons of federal officers.

Lindman reached down and hauled 'Tonio to his feet. He surveyed the newly acquired protrusion that bulged above his deputy's eye. Turning, he looked at the inspector's swollen lip. Uttering what was surely another Norwegian profanity, he grabbed 'Tonio's arm with one hand and Polanski's with the other.

"Go down to the kitchen and see if you two can't make up a couple of ice packs without getting your fingers frozen to the ice trays. I'm sure Mrs. James won't mind." His tone of voice implied that she'd better not.

With Lindman's attention temporarily focused elsewhere, Raul slipped over to Charles. "Are you all right, Sheriff?"

"I'll live," he said, glancing at the others. Dr. Hagan still looked like a spectator at a play, relaxed and anxious for the next act. Bob James was more interested in glaring at Dr. Hagan than looking at Raul, while David Lessing slumped against the wall, his eyes closed.

Lindman said, "That's a real interesting question for

a man who just arrived to ask." He rubbed his jaw and looked at Raul. "Yes, sir, real interesting. Was the sheriff out cold when you first got here, Trujillo?" he asked suddenly and smiled when he saw the deputy stiffen. "Now suppose you tell me what happened."

Charles leaned over and pressed his hand against his stomach. He wished just once that he could feel divided loyalties without his belly hurting. As a lawyer, he knew Raul shouldn't answer any questions, even informally. As a sheriff, and more specifically as a Union County deputy sheriff, he couldn't tell him so. But there was a way to serve both his duties without favoring either one.

"Lindman, the *Miranda* decision. Read him his rights."

"His rights! Damn it, Matthews, he's not under arrest, not for this crime anyway."

"It's all right, Sheriff." Raul's voice sounded tired as he shifted his eyes to Lindman and straightened his shoulders. "No one would give me a ride. I must have walked two or three miles before a trucker stopped and he only took me as far as Capulin Village." He paused and wiped his forehead, his hand trembling. "It must be five or six miles from the village to the hotel, and I walked every step of the way. There were no cars, just the dark. It's darker here at night than in the Panhandle. All the extinct volcanoes blocking the moonlight, I guess, and Capulin was the worst one. It was always there. First in front of me, then beside me, and finally behind me. And then there were all the chunks of lava jutting up from the ground, and they were black, too, and cast shadows."

"He's talking about the 'squeeze-ups,' " murmured Dr. Hagan. "Weak places in the strata where molten lava squeezed through the ground like toothpaste."

Lindman frowned at the doctor, then turned back to Raul. "When did you finally get here?"

62

Raul shivered. "I saw the lights of the hotel and I ran. There was no one downstairs, but I heard voices up here. I climbed the stairs and listened outside the door. I heard the sheriff ask who had hit him. I was scared—I started to hide in Enrique's room, but then I realized I should show myself."

"That room's more popular than a one-girl whorehouse on a Saturday night," commented Lindman. "So when did you call me?"

"I didn't," said Raul.

"Then who did?" asked Lindman. "You're the only one who knew Matthews was a sheriff."

"No," said Charles quietly. "My room was searched. Someone else knew I was a sheriff."

"Lawyer, sheriff, it doesn't make any difference," said Mary James firmly. "What were you doing in Armijo's room? Sheriff Lindman locked that room and took the key. He said it was . . . " She groped for a word.

"Sealed," said Charles automatically.

"Yes, that was it. So how did you get in?"

"I'm sorta interested in knowing that, too," interjected Lindman.

"I, uh, have ways," said Charles vaguely. "More to the point, how did the other person get in? How many keys are there to the door?"

Bob James scratched his head. "There was just one, and the sheriff took it. When we bought this place, it was kinda run down. Been empty for several years. We never have found all the keys. We finally had a locksmith come over from Clayton and make new ones. The guests like to have a key to their rooms."

"You don't have duplicates?" interrupted Charles.

"Of course, but Armijo took his key with him."

"What about a master key?"

Bob scratched his head again. "No. The guest just

leaves his key at the desk whenever he goes out and picks it up again when he comes back."

Mary James interrupted, her eyes looking distended in a pale face. "Now listen here, Sheriff Matthews, if that's who you really are. It doesn't matter if there were a hundred keys to that door, you had no business in that room. You may be somebody in Texas, but around here you're just a trespasser, and I want you out of this hotel." She gestured at Raul. "And take that criminal with you."

Charles clenched his teeth. He was beginning to dislike Mary James very much indeed. "I am also a deputy of Clayton, New Mexico, duly sworn in this afternoon. That makes this hotel and everyone in it my business."

"Wrong, Matthews; it makes it my business." Lindman stood with his hands on his hips, the heavy silver mounting of his ring gleaming in the dim ceiling light. "You are my deputy, and attacking you is the same thing as attacking me." He looked at Mary James, and for a second Charles thought he could detect fear in the woman's pale blue eyes. "Mrs. James," Lindman continued, "I'm declaring this hotel a crime scene. That means that Matthews and I will be here until we finish our investigation. Whenever that may be," he added, going to the door.

" 'Tonio!" he bellowed, sticking his head out the doorway. Charles would've sworn the old hotel shuddered. "Polanski! You two get on up here." He leaned against the door frame, crossed his arms, and waited until the two men appeared, each pressing an improvised ice pack—ice cubes wrapped in old dish towels—to various portions of their faces.

Lindman closed his eyes for a second, whether in prayer, or in an attempt to garner whatever patience he might have left, Charles didn't know. " 'Tonio, take these people downstairs and keep them company until Matthews and I are ready to talk to them."

Polanski removed the ice pack from his lip as the hotel's owners and guests filed past. "What's the meaning of this, Sheriff Lindman? We already have statements from them."

Lindman walked to the bed and offered his hand to Charles. "Think you can take a short walk, Sheriff, say as far as the next room? I want to know what in the hell is in there that's worth killing for."

Polanski followed them, waving his ice pack like a baton. "I demand to know what's going on, Lindman. In my opinion you have mismanaged this whole investigation, and—"

"You're right, Inspector. For once. I read those statements again this afternoon, and somebody's been leading me around by the nose like a yearling calf."

Charles grasped Lindman's shoulder to keep his balance. He felt sick and light-headed, and the other man's voice kept fading in and out. He drew a deep breath and forced himself to think. "You noticed that none of them have alibis?"

Lindman glanced at him ruefully. "Not a damn one of them. They all heard Trujillo and his cousin arguing, they all live in this hotel, they all knew where Armijo was going. They were all sleeping that night. Or so they say. With no desk clerk downstairs, there's no proof at all that one of them didn't take a little walk down to Capulin with an atl-atl and send Enrique Armijo to his reward prematurely."

Charles opened his mouth, but Lindman held up his hand. "That doesn't mean that Trujillo's off the hook; it just means everybody else is on it with him."

Charles's eyebrows drew together, and he let go of Lindman's shoulder. "Damn it, do you honestly believe that a deputy sheriff could be so inept that he would leave a murder weapon in his room, that he'd fail to provide himself with an alibi, and that he'd be so stupid as to threaten the victim in front of several witnesses?"

Polanski lifted the ice pack away from his mouth again. "If you state the problem that way, it doesn't sound reasonable, does it? Of course, studies show that the average IQ of a criminal is very low. It's possible he didn't think of those things."

Charles doubled up his fist, and Lindman grabbed his arm. "Relax, Matthews; you just can't knock any sense into some people. Now turn around and tell me if this room is exactly the way it was before you kissed the floor with your face."

Charles stood in the doorway of Armijo's room and carefully compared it to his memory of the fleeting glance he'd had before he'd made the acquaintance of a rabbit stick. "I think it's the same. No, wait a minute; the window's open."

Lindman walked across the room to the window. "No screen, and a nice big tree rubbing up against the outside wall. Now what does that tell us?"

"Whoever hit me didn't leave through the door."

"And why do you suppose he didn't?"

Charles grinned. "Because Mrs. James was pounding on the ceiling with her broom."

Lindman grinned back. "Meaning that whoever hit you didn't have time to find whatever the hell he was looking for."

"Or he'd already found it and it was small enough to put in his pocket," interrupted Polanski.

"Ever take any positive thinking seminars, Inspector?" asked Lindman.

The FBI man frowned. "No, I'm sure I haven't."

"I didn't think so," said Lindman.

"Whatever it was, they didn't find it," said Charles suddenly.

Polanski looked around with distaste. "I certainly don't understand how you can be certain. Everything is so—so untidy."

Charles cocked an eyebrow. Somehow he should've guessed Polanski would use a word like "untidy." "This wasn't a careful search. It was done in a hurry and probably by someone who was desperate. He didn't replace anything, just threw it on the floor."

He walked to an old table in the corner. It held a portable typewriter, a gooseneck lamp, and a stack of paper. "Whoever it was was reading through these sheets and throwing them on the floor. There's still twenty-five or thirty sheets in this stack. They're numbered, so we can check to see if all of them are in the room, but I'll take odds they are. This is the point at which I interrupted. The searcher hadn't finished going through these sheets and hadn't looked through that old dresser over there."

Lindman knelt on the floor, reading one of the sheets of paper and frowning. He picked up another sheet, skimmed it, and looked up at Charles. "This is a scientific report of some kind on the dig. There's a lot of descriptions of arrow heads or whatever, even some drawings. I don't see why anyone'd hit you over the head for this."

Polanski was examining the drawers in the dresser, removing underwear, T-shirts with various company logos over the pocket or on the sleeve, a bottle of very expensive whiskey, and a ragged-looking rucksack. Flipping it open, he pulled out several spiral-bound notebooks about half the size of the ordinary piece of stationery. He sneezed and absently wiped his nose on the very wet ice pack. Opening one of the notebooks, he dropped the ice pack altogether.

"Sheriff Lindman! Sheriff Matthews!" he shouted, waving the notebook in the air. "A journal, a very private one judging from the page I just read where he's describing an assignation with a young lady."

Lindman ripped it out of Polanski's hand and started to read. " 'F. came again tonight. Really an exquisite woman, and cleaner than her companions. Of course I demand it. Dirty feet and hands are uncouth and the sign of an uncivilized savage. Am debating taking her with me when I leave, at least for a short while. It would be worth the inconvenience of her ignorance just to watch D.'s reaction. It would be the perfect put-down for the bastard. And he deserves retribution for his wild accusations. If he dares to speak out against me again, his attacks would be attributed to jealousy. I must be more careful in the future. He could have ruined me.' "

Lindman looked up at Charles. "Cold blooded little bastard, wasn't he? Whoever F. is had a narrow escape."

"And David Lessing, and I think we can assume D. is Lessing, had a very good motive for murder."

"Sheriffs!" cried Polanski, his use of the plural making Charles feel like one-half of a burlesque act. "Listen. 'Started the excavation today. The good doctor was here for the occasion and informed me that he will be spending as much time at the dig as his "many duties" allow. What is his purpose? Could D. be filling those enormous ears with rumors about the Colorado dig and its aftermath? Those two are quite close, and the good doctor didn't believe my story. He, more than D., is dangerous. I must be careful.' "

Polanski looked up. "Not a very admirable individual."

"How much do you know about Armijo's reputation and what he was doing here?" Charles asked Lindman.

The Clayton sheriff lifted his Stetson and ran his fingers through his hair. "Not much," he admitted. "There was a lot of noise in the paper when the dig started. Reopening the Folsom Man site, newspaper reporters all over the place, even the TV stations from Santa Fe and Albuquerque sent crews. You couldn't turn around without seeing a picture of Armijo with a toothy smile, holding a trowel or a little brush. He never said anything about that kid Lessing being up here digging around for a couple of months. Hell, Lessing and old Bob James must have dug up half a ton of dirt before the almighty Armijo ever showed up. Some of the old timers around here thought the dig was a waste of time. A team of archeologists dug around that site for three years back in 1926. Couldn't be much left to find. So I can't really figure what Armijo was doing up here other than no good."

Charles grinned. "So you didn't know much about him."

Lindman shrugged. "I know the type, that's all. If he ever said 'thank you,' I'll bet he made it sound like he did someone a favor. He was one of those folks who always starts his sentences with 'I.' Probably didn't think there was anybody else important enough to talk about."

"Exactly the kind of person who invites murder," said Charles, gathering up the typed sheets of paper and retrieving the notebooks from Polanski. "And judging from just two entries in these journals, he was inviting it from more than one person." He looked at Lindman, his brown eyes hostile. "Why wasn't this room searched before now? Why weren't these notebooks found and read? If you had done that, maybe you wouldn't have been so damn quick to arrest Raul. Were you trying to impress the FBI, Lindman? Or make a case in a hurry so you could get the federal authorities out of your county?"

"Just a damn minute, Matthews—"

"I searched the room."

Polanski's voice was so soft that Charles almost didn't

hear it. He whirled on the inspector. "What did you say?"

Polanski sneezed and grabbed the wet dish towel to blow his nose, scattering melting ice cubes over the floor. He sniffed and looked up. "I said I searched the room."

Charles's profanity was short, explicit, and commonly found on bathroom walls. Polanski abruptly backed up until he bumped into the dresser. "I'm very well trained in search methods, but just as I got to this side of the room I heard Sheriff Lindman shout that he'd found the murder weapon." He wiped his forehead with the dish towel. "I never came back to finish the search. Not good procedure, I know, but it seemed unnecessary—at the time," he added defensively.

"It seemed unnecessary," repeated Charles softly. Suddenly all the frustration of the day, from the confrontation with Angie to the sight of Raul locked in jail, found a suitable target. "You damn two-bit bureaucrat," he roared as he doubled up his fist and gave the inspector a matched pair of split lips.

10

POLANSKI SAT ON one side of Charles's bed, pressing a
fresh ice pack to his mouth, while Charles sat on the
other side, Lindman's bandana wrapped around his
bleeding knuckles. A rickety wooden chair, which was
old when the first pack mule came down the Santa Fe
Trail, had been commandeered from the dining room
and was occupied by Dr. Hagan.

He looked like a pyramid as he perched on the edge
of the chair, his thick short legs spread wide, his large
hands resting on his knees. He shifted, and an ominous
creaking broke the silence. "Hope the hotel has a good
liability policy," he said with a chuckle. "I'm a little
broad across the beam to be sitting on anything smaller
than a stadium bleacher seat."

He grinned and watched as Polanski gingerly touched
his swollen mouth. "You run into a door, Inspector?"

Polanski glared at him. "Hmm," he mumbled from
behind his ice pack.

Dr. Hagan tilted his head to one side and studied
Charles's hand. "Hit the same door, Sheriff?"

Charles clenched his fist and welcomed the stinging
pain it caused. Hitting a fellow lawman, and an FBI
agent at that, had to rank near the top of the list of
incredibly stupid, unprofessional, *juvenile* things to do.
He didn't really remember getting back to his room, but
he did recall hearing Lindman using tact, then blackmail, to prevent the inspector from filing assault charges,
something about not mentioning Polanski's inadequate

search methods to the FBI in return for his forgetting about being knocked ass over elbows by a Texas county sheriff.

He rubbed his eyes, then looked at Dr. Hagan. "I'm too tired for levity, Doctor, so if you'd just give me some background information on this dig and a quick résumé of Armijo's character, I'd appreciate it."

Dr. Hagan raised an eyebrow. "Armijo's character?"

"Yes, damn it," snapped Charles, then stopped and took a deep breath. "I apologize, Doctor."

The doctor waved a hand. "No need to. If you feel as bad as you look, I shouldn't think your temper's in too good a shape either. Actually, I wasn't trying to be obstreperous, merely surprised. I expected to be asked times and places, you know, the where-were-you-when-the-foul-deed-was-done sort of thing."

Charles smiled at the doctor's obvious disappointment. "According to Mary James you were just coming out of your room. Besides, I have a good reason for believing that whatever you may have done, you didn't, uh, whack me on the head."

"Oh, and why not?"

"Because my assailant escaped the room by climbing out the window and down a convenient tree." Charles mentally crossed his fingers. They couldn't prove that, but it was the only explanation for the open window.

The doctor chuckled. "Don't exactly have the figure for climbing trees, do I?" He sobered and slapped his knees. "All right, I'll answer your questions. How much do you know about Folsom Man?"

Charles shrugged his shoulders. "I know that the term refers to a primitive Indian tribe and was chosen because the first discovery of its existence was made just a few miles from Folsom, New Mexico. From here, in other words."

"You're wrong in a couple of respects. Folsom Man

doesn't refer to a tribe; it more correctly refers to a culture. 'Tribe' implies a certain governmental organization of some sort, a cohesive unit consisting of several families, perhaps even clans. We have no evidence to support that, and a lot to dispute it. The Paleo-Indian of that time probably traveled in extended family units. Folsom Man projectile points, which are quite distinctive by the way, have been found from Wyoming to Southern New Mexico. Now either it was a hell of a big tribe, or they traveled extensively without benefit of trains, planes, or even horses. Much more accurate to use the term 'culture,' which refers to the material remains of a group of people that represent traits they had in common. To put it more simply, a culture is a level of civilization upon which succeeding levels may be built. When our remote ancestor learned to control fire, he laid the foundation for a more advanced culture. Man could now cook his food, heat his cave, frighten away wild animals. Whatever culture invented the wheel made the development of modern transportation possible."

"Sheriff Lindman, I must object. None of this information is important. Armijo wasn't killed by a—" Polanski groped for a word—"Folsom Man," he finished.

Charles jerked around on the bed, and Polanski clapped both hands over his mouth. "This whole case is permeated by archeology and Folsom Man. I think there's a connection between the kind of weapon used and the motive for murder."

Polanski moved his hands. "The atl-atl happened to be handy and, as a deputy, Trujillo knew a gun or knife would be easily traced. How would you trace an atl-atl? They're not sold over the counter, you know."

"Shut up," said Charles.

Polanski looked at Charles's expression and decided he would.

"To continue," said Dr. Hagan, as though he'd never been interrupted. "Your second error is the interpretation of the discovery. We knew primitive man had reached New Mexico; what we didn't know, and what Folsom Man proved, was how long man had been in the New World. Prior to the Folsom Man discovery, it was pretty well agreed that man had been in the New World only about four thousand years, give or take a few hundred. But at the Folsom Man site, a projectile point was found embedded in an animal, authoritatively believed to have been extinct for ten thousand years. We know now that there were older cultures than Folsom Man, the Clovis for example, but none have caught the imagination like Folsom Man. That single projectile point embedded in a *Bison antiquus figginsi* revolutionized archeological thinking."

The doctor's voice had taken on a lecturing note, and Charles could imagine him in a college classroom. "We know several things about Folsom Man. First of all, he made a lethal but aesthetically beautiful projectile point; second, he was a skilled hunter capable of killing two-thousand-pound bison with those projectile points; third, he was almost certainly nomadic, as are all cultures who live on big game; fourth, he skinned the bison, probably for clothing; fifth he was *Homo sapiens,* a modern man. We're not talking about a walking apelike creature, but a man you could dress in modern clothes, drop on the nearest Indian reservation, and no one would look at him twice. He might be shorter, probably was, but other than that he was like you and me."

The doctor chuckled and recrossed his legs. "Of course, his standard of living was lower. He lived in caves when he could find them, dressed in skins, was subject to dental and general health problems that we have conquered. He slaughtered far more animals than he could possibly eat at one time. That is not to say he was killing for the sake of killing, like so many modern hunters do; it was a matter of hunting methods. He would stampede whole herds over a cliff, rush down and kill the animals not already dead, and butcher them on the spot. What the clan could not eat and were not able to carry away was simply left. Techniques of preserving and storing food are not usually associated with nomadic big-game hunters. They would eat the meat for a month, that being the maximum length of time it remained edible."

Dr. Hagan was silent for a moment. "Mind you, I wouldn't care to eat month-old bison meat, but then I'm not Folsom Man."

Lindman, who had been leaning on the wall, broke in. "What's all this got to do with digging the old Folsom Man site again?"

Both Dr. Hagan's eyebrows rose at once. "But we're not; we're actually excavating an area that overlooked the ravine ten thousand years ago. No point in going over old ground. So to speak," he added with a chuckle. "We can't seem to make that clear to the press, though. They keep writing the most inaccurate drivel about the original site and new finds expected."

Charles interrupted. Hagan had done a lot of talking, but didn't seem to be any closer to answering any questions than he was ten minutes before. "But why? Why was Armijo here? Damn it, we've got to know. We can't separate the location of a murder from the act of murder because unless we're dealing with a random killer, there's usually a tentative cause-and-effect relationship. It's almost a cliché that if a victim hadn't been in a particular place at a particular time, he'd still be alive. You've done a lot of talking about the importance of the original site, but you've said nothing about the new dig."

"You know how it is with old men, and most particularly professors, we ramble a lot." The doctor grinned, then cleared his throat when he observed the three impatient men facing him. "Hmm. Well, the reason for the new dig is Bob James, or rather something he found."

"A skeleton?" guessed Charles, that being the most exciting find he could think of.

"Ah, Sheriff, that's been a secret dream of mine. To find a skeleton of Folsom Man, complete with a cache of projectile points buried with him. Unfortunately, one has never been found. In fact, we don't have a skull, a jaw bone, or even the joint of a finger from Folsom Man. I'm almost willing to agree with a colleague of mine who swears they must have cremated their dead. An interesting theory, but impossible to prove."

"Doctor," said Charles through gritted teeth, "would you get on with it?"

"What? Oh, yes, what Bob James found. A balance stone, gentlemen, a rather nice one at that." He sat back and beamed like a parent who's just given his child a much wished-for toy.

"What the hell is a balance stone?" asked Lindman.

Dr. Hagan sighed. His children had disappointed him. "It's a polished stone fastened to an atl-atl as either a weight or a fetish. Personally, I think it was used to give the atl-atl greater throwing power. Still, some believe it was a fetish stone, strictly for ceremonial reasons. Any time archeologists can't decide the purpose of an artifact, they call it a ceremonial object. We've assigned so many ceremonial objects to the primitive American that he'd have had to spend twelve hours a day practicing his religion to use them all."

"And what is so important about this, uh, balance stone?"

"If there is a balance stone connected with a Folsom Man site, and found in the same stratum, then that

76

would go a long way toward proving that he had developed the atl-atl."

Polanski removed his ice pack. The swelling was subsiding in the lower lip, but his upper lip protruded so far that he looked a little like a camel. "Is that important?" he asked.

Dr. Hagan looked aghast. "Important! Young man, was the development of the atom bomb important? The atl-atl was its primitive equivalent. A tall, strong hunter may be able to throw a spear fifty to seventy-five feet. A dart thrown with an atl-atl may travel two hundred to three hundred feet and still be lethal. Think of the advantages. You wouldn't have to be as close to your prey, reducing the danger of injury. And remember, with no antibiotics, a simple cut could become infected and lead to death. The old business of primitive man being a healthy man is hogwash. Primitive man had a life expectancy of twenty-five to thirty years, and most of those years were physically painful. From tooth decay if nothing else."

The doctor started to grin, but the look on Charles's face persuaded him that he'd better summarize quickly or he might be looking for his own ice pack. "In short, gentlemen, the discovery of a balance stone would be almost as noteworthy as the discovery of the missing link."

"Now, Dr. Hagan," Lindman said, "If I understand you, Armijo was here because Bob James found a rock."

Dr. Hagan grimaced at Lindman's description of a valuable artifact as a common rock. "I guess you could put it that way," he said dryly.

"What about his character, Dr. Hagan?" asked Charles.

"I don't like to speak ill of the dead. . . . "

"Don't worry about it," interrupted Lindman. "Someone thought so ill of him alive that they skewered him like a shish kebab."

The professor tapped a broad finger on his broad knee. "Someone? I take it then that these questions are not just to satisfy our Texas sheriff that everything was handled correctly, but that you also may be having doubts that cousin Raul is the guilty party."

"Just answer Matthews," said Lindman, his bland voice giving no indication he'd even heard Hagan's comment.

"Armijo was brilliant, flamboyant, impatient, caustic, ego-centered, absolutely ruthless when it came to his own reputation. He was an unmitigated bastard, thoroughly detested by everyone who'd ever been a target of one of his attacks."

"David Lessing indicated that everyone had a motive for murdering Armijo. Were you ever one of his targets?" asked Charles quietly.

"In layman's terms, as chairman of the department, I was his boss. I am also a very methodical scientist; I'm not given to flights of fancy based on insufficient evidence. And in my own way, I'm just as ruthless as he. In short, it would have been most unwise for him to have picked me as a target. You'll have to pick another suspect, gentlemen; he simply wasn't a threat to me."

"What happened to Armijo on the Colorado dig?" asked Charles suddenly.

For a split second Dr. Hagan's pupils dilated and his jovial old Saint Nicholas expression vanished. Then he blinked, and Charles wondered if he'd really hit a vulnerable spot, or if the professor was merely surprised at the shift in questioning.

Then Dr. Hagan rubbed his jaw, and Charles knew instinctively the professor was going to be selective with the truth. Charles had questioned too many suspects to be wrong.

"The Colorado dig was an archeologist's dream. Bones of almost a hundred bison were found, projectile points, a campsite with a hearth. Armijo published a paper on the dig that was reprinted in several journals."

"What else, Doctor?" asked Charles. He wished he'd had time to read all of Armijo's journals. But he hadn't, so he'd have to bluff. "We know something happened at that dig, and you've as much as admitted it, so you might as well tell me."

Dr. Hagan looked like an aging, innocent cherub. "I haven't admitted anything, Sheriff."

Charles grabbed the bed post and pulled himself to his feet. The professor was a tough adversary, and he'd be damned if he'd question him from a semi-prone position. "I ask a simple question about the present dig, and I get a bird's eye view of North American archeology. I know more about Folsom Man ten thousand years ago than I need to, but I ask about a dig that Enrique Armijo led last year, and I learn exactly nothing. Now why is that, Doctor?"

"It has nothing to do with why Armijo was murdered, but I suppose you'll chew on it like a dog on a bone if I don't tell you. A graduate assistant on the dig committed suicide a few months after Armijo closed down the excavation. All that potential, all that brilliance, wasted!" He looked up at Charles. "We'll never know, of course, but I believe we lost an archeologist as great as H.W. Wormington. So I don't like to talk about the Colorado dig; it's too painful."

He rose, a massive figure who managed to retain his dignity even in a mustard-yellow bathrobe. "I never like to admit it, Sheriff, but I'm an old man and I'm tired. If you're through, I'd like to go back to bed."

Charles watched the professor leave the room, then turned to look at Lindman. "How good are your contacts on the Albuquerque police department?"

"Good enough. Why?"

Charles dropped heavily back onto the bed. "The last

time I was home, my niece was working on a class project on famous women. Her report was on H. Marie Wormington, one of the foremost archeologists of this century."

Lindman pulled on one earlobe. "So the graduate assistant was a woman."

Polanski spoke for the first time since Hagan's explanation of the dig. His lower lip was almost back to normal. "Why didn't the professor tell us that?"

"Now, that is an interesting question," said Charles.

11

"SURE YOU DON'T want one of these cold beers, Sheriff Matthews?" Bob James asked, gesturing at a six pack so cold the bottles looked frosted. "I figured if we were going to be talking much, we might want something to keep our throats from drying out."

Charles managed not to shudder. The thought of cold beer hitting an already rebellious stomach was enough to give his mouth an aftertaste of bile. "No, thanks, Mr. James, I'm fine." He wasn't though. His head still hurt, he was nauseous, and his knuckles stung. Add exhaustion to the list, and he felt like a puppet with most of its strings broken.

"I'll take one," said Polanski, bouncing off the bed and reaching for a bottle. "Lots of breweries around Chicago. I was practically raised on beer. According to statistics, beer is . . ."

Lindman interrupted the inspector in mid-statistic. "So you found a rock, did you, Bob? Did you expect it would cause more fuss than a two-headed calf?"

Bob James leaned forward in the old wooden chair. His eyes seemed almost to shoot sparks. "Fuss? This is nothing. I find one of the most important artifacts in the last forty years, and what do I get? One graduate student. For something this important, they should have sent in a real team, experts in all fields. And the timing! We should've been digging all summer. Hell, no. 'Wait,' they said. So David Lessing and I didn't get started until August. Damn it, the ground's going to start to freeze pretty quick, and then we can't dig at all. And Dr. High-and-Mighty Enrique Armijo doesn't show up until a month later. Then he tries to bar me from the dig. 'Listen,' I tell him; 'this is private property and the owner is a friend of mine. He wants me here to protect his interests. I go, and you'll go. So put that in your Ph.D. and see how you like it' 'Course I was lying. The owner wouldn't throw out an archeological team, not that he could anyway. The state could force him to allow access to the site. But, damn it, I was mad. Who did he think he was anyway? Some very important discoveries have been made by amateurs. Richard Wetherill discovered Mesa Verde, and he didn't have a Ph.D."

James's eyes took on a fanatical expression. "They can try to cheat me if they want to, but I'll win. I'll prove Folsom Man had the atl-atl, in spite of their half-assed dig. And all Armijo wanted to do was chase the Leader's woman. I tell you . . . "

"What's her name?" asked Charles sharply.

"Er, Faith."

Charles and Lindman exchanged a look, and Polanski lowered his second bottle of beer and stared at the hotel owner. The F. in the journal was identified.

"How did the Leader feel about that?" asked Lindman.

Bob James leaned back in his chair. "He didn't like it, I can tell you that. He and Armijo got into a fight about it. But then he didn't like Armijo anyway, says he was, well, bad medicine. He always said the spirit of Folsom Man would curse him."

He took a long drink of beer. "It was David that was really bothered about the girl. That boy spends a lot of time hanging around the Skin People. He says they're interesting, but I figure the most interesting thing about them, far as a young fellow is concerned, is Faith. She's kinda quiet and sad acting, but she sure is a looker."

"Who are these Skin People?" Charles asked, ignoring

Lindman's sharp look. He knew the Union County sheriff would know everything about the band up to and probably including what they ate for breakfast on any given morning, but he wanted to hear Bob James's opinion.

The hotel manager rubbed his bald spot and considered Charles's question. "They're interesting folks. I guess people around here don't like them much, but they mind their own business. The Leader says that modern civilization is corrupt and destructive, that man has to return to the natural way or die. So they try to live just like Folsom Man did. They hunt and use the hides for clothes. They make their own projectile points, damn good ones, too, and some of them are real accurate with an atl-atl. They got respect, you know. I think that's why the Leader didn't like Armijo. He didn't have respect. A projectile point was just a piece of flint to him; he never thought much about the people who made it. They were just savages to him."

"So the Leader thinks Folsom Man had developed the atl-atl," asked Charles.

"He's a real smart man, the Leader. He knows so much about Folsom Man, he can almost think like one. He's the one that put me on to the campsite. He said that Folsom Man probably built a fire and had a feast on all the bison meat they had that day. What they couldn't eat, they carried off. Even if their women and younguns weren't with them, the hunters would want to eat some of that meat. We walked along the ridge above the ravine and just guessed lucky. Of course, erosion had lowered it some, so we didn't have to trench very far before I found the balance stone."

James grinned, reached down, and got another beer. "Yes, sir, it was a lucky day that I met the Leader."

"You hadn't know him long?" asked Polanski, anticipating Charles's question.

"No, his band moved into a cave up near Johnson Mesa just a couple weeks before I saw him. I went up to see them when a rancher friend of mine told me they killed one of his cows with an atl-atl."

"I bet they're popular with the ranchers around here," remarked Charles dryly.

James shrugged. "They paid him for it, better than market price, so he didn't care."

"They have money?" asked Polanski, interrupting his beer drinking again.

James rubbed his head again. "I never thought about it, but I guess they do. They paid the rancher who owns the land where the cave is. That's why he's never called the sheriff to arrest them for trespassing."

"The Leader certainly told you a lot," said Lindman. "More than I could get out of him when I went out to make his acquaintance." He looked at Charles. "You know how it is. I didn't want some cult moving into my county without my checking them out."

"The Leader didn't tell me that," interjected James. "The rancher did. I dig a lot on his ranch, so I know him pretty well. Found some fine points on his place, too. Did you notice my collection downstairs, Sheriff Matthews?" he asked with the pride of a small boy showing off his arrowhead collection.

"I could hardly miss it," said Charles, thinking of the mounted projectile points, scrapers, flint knives, and other artifacts that covered every available wall. In fact, the whole hotel looked like an armory, prehistoric style.

Bob James leaned forward again, a petulant droop to his mouth. "Dr. Hagan curses every time he looks at it. He says I'm looting prehistory. But I'm not; I'm a guardian."

"Speaking of Dr. Hagan, isn't he helping with the dig?" asked Charles.

"He's not here all the time. Let's see, he came with

Armijo when we started to deepen the trench, and he was here last week. Then he went back to Albuquerque early Saturday morning. Matter of fact, he was gone when I got up. That was the morning the rangers found Armijo's body. He didn't get back 'til late Saturday night. I heard he helped at the autopsy."

"Anything you want to add to the statement you made about the events just prior to the murder?" asked Lindman.

"You mean about Raul and the argument? No, I can't tell you anything else. Mary made me a cup of her herbal tea, and I slept like a baby. Sherman's army could've marched by my door, and I wouldn't have heard them."

Lindman waved his hand. "I think that's all, Bob. You and Mary go on to bed. We'll talk to David Lessing, then I think Matthews here had better turn in. I've seen corpses that looked better than he does."

Charles waited until the door closed behind Bob James, then pulled himself to his feet again. He walked the few steps to Lindman, clenching and unclenching his fists. His skin felt too small for his body, a sign that his temper was ready to erupt, and he took a deep breath. "Damn you, Lindman. You never said a word about Hagan leaving on Saturday, and he didn't mention it in his statement. Do you have any proof he didn't leave Friday night after everyone else was in bed? Do you have any proof that he didn't murder Armijo?"

Lindman flushed, and his blue eyes took on a chipped ice look. "Do you see Hagan walking five miles to Capulin, creeping up behind Armijo, and burying an atl-atl in his chest? My God, the man is sixty-five years old and must weight three hundred pounds."

"He wouldn't have to 'creep up' behind him. Hagan himself said a man could throw a spear three hundred feet using an atl-atl. Now why didn't you tell me about his leaving?"

"I figured you knew how to read a statement. You could've looked at the time at the top and realized we questioned him later than the others. Now if you think I'm trying to railroad your deputy into prison, just say so."

It was Charles's turn to flush. Lindman was right; he could've looked at the times. "I'm just saying you were too quick to arrest Raul."

"Sheriff, I'm gonna say this one time. You ain't got any business investigating this crime because you're too close. You can't see the forest for the trees. If Raul Trujillo weren't your deputy, and you were in my place, you'd have arrested him, too. He has motive, opportunity, and no alibi. I haven't heard anything tonight to make me change my mind except that the more I find out about Armijo, the more I think your deputy ought to plead justifiable homicide."

"Why did you recommend bail?"

Lindman took his Stetson off and studied it as if he'd never seen it before. "I'm kinda like the rancher that finds a calf mauled and coyote sign around it. He gets to looking closer and he finds a lot of other sign, too, and all of a sudden he ain't so sure the coyote's to blame. At first all the sign pointed to your deputy. And it still does. But I'm finding other sign now, and a man's life is worth more than a coyote's. I've got to be sure."

He look up, and Charles saw his own fears reflected in Lindman's eyes. They all faced it, every sheriff, every cop: that secret fear that some day they might make a mistake, that fatigue or pressure or superficial evidence or their own personal prejudice would lead them to arrest an innocent man.

Polanski set his beer bottle on the washstand. "This is the most unorthodox investigation I've ever been involved in. I don't know whether I'm dealing with county sheriffs or Indian trackers."

Lindman slapped his Stetson back on. "In New Mexico, sometimes you have to be both." Opening the door, he leaned out and bellowed. " 'Tonio! Send Lessing up!"

He turned around to Charles. "Time to interview another set of tracks."

"All I ever wanted to do was investigate forgeries. Instead, what do I get? Tracks, coyotes, projectile points, digs, hippies running around acting like prehistoric Indians." Polanski wandered back to the bed, retrieved his ice pack, and flopped down on the bed.

David Lessing came in, and Lindman waved him toward the venerable wooden chair. "Sit down, son, but carefully, or that damn thing's gonna fall to pieces."

Sitting down, Lessing stretched his legs out, crossed his arms, and stared at Lindman. "I didn't kill Armijo and I didn't assault the sheriff."

Lindman took a step closer until Lessing had to tilt his head back to see his face. "But you did call me tonight, didn't you? To tell me Matthews had been assaulted?"

Lessing lowered his head and looked at the floor. His lips were pressed together so tightly they had lost their color.

Lindman leaned down and caught the younger man's chin and jerked his head up. "Don't get the sulks with me, son. We ain't talking about whether you went and stole a car and went joy riding on Saturday night. We're talking about somebody shoving a spear into another man's chest. Now you answer my question."

"What if I did?"

Lindman let go of his chin and stepped back. "And you searched the sheriff's room? Didn't you?"

Lessing's glance darted away quickly, ricocheted off Charles's face, and finally settled on examining the frayed knee of his Levi's. "I must have if I knew he was a sheriff."

Charles started to interrupt, but closed his mouth instead. Sometimes listening to lies was almost as informative as listening to the truth.

"So that scared you, didn't it, knowing there was another sheriff here who was going to be asking questions all over again, poking into people's lives? Is that when you decided to search Armijo's room, too? You were going to make sure there was nothing there that might lead back to you?"

"I didn't search Armijo's room!" cried Lessing.

Lindman's voice rolled on, his Norwegian accent transformed from harmless to dangerous in some way that Charles couldn't understand. "I figure Sheriff Matthews interrupted your search; and you grabbed that rabbit stick off its mounting, hit him, then got scared and shinnied out the window and down the tree. You were just coming in from a short walk when Mrs. James saw you, a short walk around the house."

"No, I didn't hit him! I was just coming back from"—the pause was almost imperceptible—"a walk. I came upstairs with Mary, and we found him. While she and Dr. Hagan were examining him, I went back downstairs and called you."

Lindman reached down, opened Charles's suitcase, and pulled out one of Armijo's notebooks. "This was what you were looking for."

David's whole body stiffened, then went slack. He licked his lips. "I never saw those before."

Lindman ruffled the pages. "These are Armijo's private journals. Makes real interesting reading. For instance, we know you hated Armijo because he was straying on your range. Must have been worse than a burr under your saddle to have your professor take your girl. That's what happens though; women just can't see through somebody like him. Now when you get as old as I am, you don't let things like—"

"He was a bastard! He was using her just like he did
. . ." His mouth snapped shut.

"Just like he did the girl on the Colorado dig?" asked
Lindman softly.

David jerked his head up to look at Lindman. He wet
his lips again and humped his shoulders like a child in
trouble. Charles felt a sliver of compassion. The boy
couldn't begin to hold out against Lindman. The Clayton
sheriff had too many years of experience dealing with
belligerent adolescents, and David wasn't much past
that stage.

"What happened in Colorado, David?" asked Charles.

"I wasn't on the Colorado dig," he said dully.

"But you know something about it?"

He rubbed his palms together. "I read the reports on
it, that's all."

"We know about the suicide, David," said Charles
softly.

"I'm not saying anything else." He seemed to age, his
eyes becoming old and bitter, scarred with memories.

Charles glanced at Lindman, who nodded uncon-
sciously in agreement. They both knew the pendulum
had swung. No matter what they asked, David Lessing
would say nothing more.

Lindman closed the door behind David Lessing,
took off his Stetson, and slapped it against his leg.
"Damn it, he's lying. He's got to be! Whoever climbed
down that tree had to get back in the hotel by the front
door."

"Isn't there a back door?" asked Polanski.

"Yes." Lindman sat down on the chair. "It leads right
into the kitchen and Mary James with her broom. And
they didn't come in after she left the kitchen because
everybody was already upstairs. Except David Lessing.
And your deputy," he added with a glance at Charles.

"Raul didn't need to search my room. He knows who I am."

"Maybe Lessing searched your room, and Trujillo searched the other one," suggested Polanski.

"Sure, and it's gonna snow in July," said Lindman. "You're suggesting two different sets of suspects with the same victim in mind."

"Why not," said Charles suddenly. He got up and paced. "Everyone in this case, *except* Raul, is connected in some way with archeology. Dr. Hagan, David Lessing, Bob James—they're all involved in this Folsom Man dig. Even the Leader is involved. He's the one that selected the site where Bob James found that weight. That's one set of suspects. Everyone has a motive: Dr. Hagan and David for whatever happened on the Colorado dig; the Leader, who thinks he's Folsom Man incarnate, didn't think Armijo had the proper respect; and Bob James, who was jealous about Armijo taking over his site. It's a closed circle, a perfect setup for murder. Then Raul comes to the hotel and provides the opportunity. Here is an outsider, someone not connected with archeology, someone sure to be blamed because he has a perfect motive."

Lindman sank down on the chair. "The professor and Lessing are both hiding something about the Colorado dig, but it may not have anything to do with the murder."

Polanski cleared his throat. "It seems to me that Mr. Trujillo's motive outweighs any other's, if indeed what we've been hearing can even be construed as motives."

"I'll have to agree with Polanski," said Lindman. "All this business about archeology and some old man wearing a rotten antelope hide and believing in some kind of hocus-pocus about spirits and respect is just clouding the trail."

"But what about the weapon?" asked Charles desperately. "Even the weapon was an archeological artifact. An atl-atl, for God's sake."

Lindman got up and grasped Charles's shoulder. "We can sit here all night and make up stories about who's guilty and who's not, and it won't change a thing. I've got to have proof, damn it, evidence that'll stand up in court. I can't drop charges against your deputy without it."

Charles jerked away and turned his back. "What about the attack on me, Lindman? How does that fit into your case?"

"It doesn't, and that's why I'm still standing around here instead of being home in bed."

Polanski cleared his throat. "It seems to be that we're theorizing without facts. Perhaps the best course of action is to read Armijo's journals."

Lindman clapped the inspector on the back. "By God, Polanski, the FBI comes through in a pinch, doesn't it. Let's see what the dead man can tell us about his own murder."

"And there's another set of tracks around the victim, Lindman," said Charles.

Lindman cocked an eyebrow. "The Leader?"

"And his followers. According to their statements, they neither saw nor heard anything of the murder. Just like the three monkeys: see no evil, hear no evil, do no evil."

"They smell like monkeys," said Lindman. "I had to stand upwind to question them."

"I'll wear a clothes pin," replied Charles sourly.

12

SHERIFF LINDMAN LAID down the last notebook and rubbed his eyes. "I'm surprised Armijo wasn't murdered sooner. According to him no one else was fit to breathe the same air. He referred to the Leader as 'a subspecies of Homo sapiens.' He even called Mary James a nosy old woman and told her to stay out of his room."

"I'm surprised she didn't take after him with a broom," said Charles dryly.

"He certainly was explicit about his, uh, physical needs. I've read cleaner pornography than some of the entries concerning his activities with Faith," remarked Polanski, his face as red as the end of his nose.

"Why, Inspector, I didn't know you read anything but FBI reports," said Lindman with a grin.

Polanski blushed, stuttered, then buried his face in his soggy ice pack.

"Yet he dismissed Raul with a single entry," said Charles. "And it was only a remark that Raul was a stupid oaf, not worthy to be his relative. That's mild compared to some of his epithets."

"His mother should've wrapped him in a gunnysack and dropped him in the river after he was born," said Lindman with utter disgust.

"Water pollution," muttered Polanski through his ice pack.

Lindman chuckled. "That's good, Polanski. We'll make a Westerner out of you yet." The inspector shuddered.

"There are two more references to the Colorado dig,"

said Charles. " 'Yesterday'—" he glanced at the date at the top of the page—"that was Thursday, 'we found seven projectile points and a scraper, the first hint that some sort of hide processing was done at the site. It will substantiate the Colorado finds, and I will share the credit with no one.' "

"I'll bet Bob James loved that," commented Lindman sourly.

Charles nodded. "Evidently, because Armijo mentions it later in the same entry," he continued, flipping through the pages. " 'Bob James accused me of stealing his discoveries. How dare he think that he is capable of interpreting this site? Lessing snidely asked if I thought I was still in Colorado. I must get rid of both of them.' "

"It sounds like it was Armijo who had murder in mind," remarked Lindman. "I'm surprised we didn't find Bob James or Lessing with a spear in their backs."

"*And* Dr. Hagan," said Polanski. "One of the entries is quite profane. It seems the professor refused to take Lessing and James off the dig. He also refused to send in more archeologists."

Charles yawned and rubbed eyes that now felt as if they had projectile points in them. "Polanski, how would you like to throw some weight around?"

"I beg your pardon."

"We need information, and the FBI has enough pull to get it for us quickly."

Polanski smiled, then winced as his sore mouth objected to being stretched. "I'm glad you finally admitted the FBI is good for something."

"Polanski, you're not so bad when you're not being a pain in the neck," commented Lindman.

Charles took an old envelope out of his pocket and scribbled a list. He handed it to the inspector and said tersely, "And hurry back with it, for God's sake."

Polanski took the list and nodded happily as he read

it. Then he frowned over the last item. "Textbooks on Southwestern archeology. What do you want those for? We already have two archeologists. Can't they tell you whatever you need to know?"

"Let's just say I'm interested in the subject and I'd like a third opinion."

Polanski nodded and glanced at his watch. "I'll try to be back Monday night."

Lindman tapped his watch. "It's three o'clock in the morning, Polanski. It's already Monday." He fished a set of keys out of his pocket. "Take the patrol car. And use the siren," he called after the departing inspector.

He turned back to Charles. "Hit the sack, Sheriff. I'll go tell 'Tonio to bed down your deputy, and I'll sleep in Armijo's room. Maybe his departed spirit will give me a hint as to what the hell is going on in my county."

Charles waved his hand in agreement, then sat down on the bed and began to sort out the typed pages of whatever report Armijo had been working on. Finally getting them in order, he skimmed the report, then yawned, and placed it on his bedside table. He never realized a dry scientific report could be an egotistical document. One would believe from reading it that Armijo was the only man involved on the dig. There was no mention of Dr. Hagan, David Lessing, or Bob James.

He yawned again. He'd reconsider the report in the morning and decide then if there was anything in it that might be a motive. Right now his head was pounding, his vision was blurring, and his mind was refusing to comprehend the unfamiliar scientific jargon. He'd have to read the textbooks first. He rolled over, heard the bed protest with a crackling of rope, and thought how Angie would laugh when he described his night in this museum. He sobered; for just a moment he'd forgotten. He wouldn't be sharing anything with Angie again.

He laced his fingers behind his head and stared at the

ceiling, contemplating the emptiness of the rest of his life. The pale glow of false dawn lit the room before exhaustion finally forced him to sleep.

Lindman leaned over the seat and tapped Raul on the shoulder. "Better stop at the Visitors' Center, Trujillo. The superintendent will want to know we're here." He chuckled. "To tell the truth he won't want to know. He'll start stuttering again when he sees my face."

Superintendent Hamilton didn't stutter, but he did exhibit the resigned attitude of Job waiting for another plague from God. "I know, Lindman, you don't need to tell me. You've come to close up the monument again. Mount Capulin hasn't seen this many peace officers since the time those teenagers carried a bunch of tires into the crater and set fire to them. The whole county thought Capulin was about to erupt. Were you sheriff then?"

Lindman looked uncomfortable. "Uh, no; I was still a, uh, teenager."

"The oldtimers around here still talk about it. They say the ringleader's dad nearly defoliated the trees on the cinder cone; blistered the leaves with his language. Blistered his son's behind, too. It must have been something. The dad was a Swede or something, married to a Mexican woman around here. They said he was cussing in three languages."

Charles glanced at Lindman. "Anybody you know, Sheriff?" he asked with his first grin since leaving Crawford County.

Lindman's face was the color of brick and just as rigid. "We're going up to the crater. My new deputy, Matthews here, wants to see the crime scene."

The superintendent put on his hat, and Charles wondered if Hamilton was aware that most people thought the park service copied Smokey the Bear's headgear instead of the other way around. "There's nothing left to see, thank God. Did you know we had to station a ranger at the bottom of the crater to keep people from trying to climb the sides to look for blood stains? We had three sprained ankles and a snakebite yesterday." He thought a moment and grinned. "We also had the highest visitation day in the history of the park. Over fifteen hundred people viewed Capulin. And we didn't have one visitor ask if Capulin was going to erupt like Mt. St. Helens. But still, murder is not an acceptable way to boost attendance."

Charles scooted down in the front seat and braced his knees against the dashboard in preparation for the drive up to the crater. He didn't like heights, and he didn't like admitting it so he forced himself to look out the window as the crater road spiraled two miles to the top.

"Ever been to Capulin before, Deputy Matthews?"

Charles swallowed. "Passed by it a few times."

"You must come see it when you're off-duty. Take the Crater Rim Trail. You can see five states from the highest point. There are also about one hundred recognizable volcanoes surrounding the monument. A lot of history happened around here: the Cimarron Cutoff of the Santa Fe Trail, the Folsom Man discovery . . . " He stopped and cleared his throat. "Well, I guess you know about that."

"You might say I've received quite an education in Folsom Man lately," said Charles and closed his eyes as an oncoming car passed them on the narrow road.

When they reached the top and had walked the short asphalt trail down into the crater itself, Charles was both relieved and disappointed. Relieved that he'd be on the inside lane when they drove back down, and disappointed that the superintendent was right: there wasn't anything to see except some trampled shrubs and a scorched spot on the trail at the very bottom of the crater.

Charles stuck his hands in his pockets and hunched his shoulders. The temperature hovered around forty degrees, and the wind lowered it still more. It was cold and miserable in the daylight and must have been worse at night. "Do you know where the murderer was standing?"

Lindman pointed at a spot about fifty yards away. "There, we think. It's hard to tell for sure. Those damn Skin People tramped over the place. I got a couple of dogs, but between the outdated hippies, the rangers, and my own deputies, we didn't find much. Doesn't help that there's a herd of mule deer that lives in the crater. Damn dogs led us a chase up the side. By golly, we thought we really had something, until the dogs flushed out three mule deer. The handler and I exchanged a few words, and he left."

Charles could imagine. A few words from Lindman would be enough to make most men leave. "What about Indian trackers?" he asked. "The Jarillo Apache Reservation isn't very far . . . " He stopped abruptly as Lindman's eyes rolled heavenward.

"Indians!" Lindman uttered a profanity in English, and while Charles was unfamiliar with that particular adjective being used with that particular verb, he had to admit it created a strong image. "You did say Indians, didn't you, Matthews? What do you think this is, the nineteenth century? For God's sake, the Indians around here are farmers and businessmen. They can't read sign any better than any of us white eyes who were raised in this country and are used to going hunting. Hell, my medical investigator told me more than the dogs and as much as the Indians could. Pretty smart, that kid. Does a lot of hunting himself and has learned to track with the best of them. He says the murderer stood over the body on one foot."

"What!" exclaimed Charles.

Lindman shrugged. "We figured he put his foot on Armijo to gain leverage when he was trying to pull out the foreshaft."

"God!" said Charles and swallowed.

"Yeah," agreed Lindman. "Somebody had a pretty strong stomach."

"Did you get a cast of the footprint?"

Lindman looked disgusted. "With this wind, and on this kind of terrain? You been reading too many detective stories where the murderer steps in the wet flower bed on a calm night. First off, there ain't no dirt, just a lot of bushes and shrubs. We can tell by a lot of broken twigs and some dead grass shoved in where he stood, but I could put my foot down and make the same kind of print."

Charles flushed. First his comment about the Indians, then an equally stupid remark about the footprints. He should have known better. It was next to impossible to make casts outdoors in the Panhandle and for at least one of the same reasons: the damn wind could blow away anything save a concrete block building, and it could damage that.

He changed the subject. "What about the Skin People? Did he see any of their sign around the body?"

Lindman took off his hat and scratched his head. "Yeah, it's hard to miss those moccasins; they're hard as shoe leather and the sinew thread used to sew them cuts into the ground. They came in from the same direction as Armijo and the murderer and went back the same way. We can tell 'cause we could follow a trail of bent branches and grass and pebbles that had been disturbed. Still, they're good about not leaving much sign; a whole lot better at that than they are at tanning hides. They knew that body was there, but they all said they didn't see a damn thing. Couldn't shake them from their story."

"I think the Leader and his band are lying," said Charles abruptly. Armijo's body was only about seventy-five feet from their campfire. They had to have at least heard the body fall."

"They were having some kind of a ritual with chants and so forth, probably high on some drug."

"Drugs affect your equilibrium and coordination. They couldn't have left so little sign unless they were cold sober."

Lindman's profanity was extensive, sounded imaginative, and was all in Norwegian. "Damn it," he finished in English. "I'd better retire and build furniture like my father did. But first we're going over to the Leader's cave and I'm going to tie knots in his loincloth. I never met a man so damn good at lying."

Lindman muttered all the way back up the trail and halfway down the volcano. Finally he leaned over the seat. "Drive back toward the hotel, and I'll direct you from there, Trujillo."

Bob James flagged them down halfway to the hotel. The hotel owner's fringe of hair circled his head like a sandy-colored hedge, and the whites of his eyes seemed to completely surround the iris. He stomped over to Charles's car in heavy lace-up work boots as if he was stepping on cockroaches, followed more sedately by Dr. Hagan and David Lessing. "It's those damn Skin People. They're going to ruin everything. You've got to arrest them, Sheriff Lindman; throw 'em in jail. If you don't, I'm going to fill the Leader's hind end so full of buckshot, he'll rattle when he walks."

Lindman's face turned a mottled red at the mention of the Leader and Charles wondered if he were going to offer to load the hotel owner's shotgun, but Lindman gave a regretful sigh as duty apparently outweighed personal wishes. "Slow down, Bob. Now just what have the Skin People done? Other than smell," he added.

"They won't let us get to the site. They barred the way and even started rocking my jeep. Dr. Hagan and David wanted to get out and reason with the Leader. I said hell, no, did they want to get their heads bashed in with a stone axe? I tell you, Sheriff, the Leader's gone crazy. If he were foaming at the mouth, I'd say he picked up rabies from all those half-cooked rabbits they eat. But he ain't. I just don't know what's wrong with him," he finished plaintively.

Dr. Hagan patted Bob James's shoulder. "Calm down. You're getting worked up over nothing."

Bob James turned on the professor with bared teeth. "Nothing! How can you call endangering the most important dig of the century nothing!"

"You can't call an atl-atl weight, which you should have left *in situ,* the most important find of the century. We can't even verify the strata where you found it so we can get geological dating. No one will just take your word for it. Even Figgins, when he was excavating the original Folsom Man site, was disbelieved until he found a projectile point actually embedded in the bison remains. He left it alone and sent telegrams to all the leading archeologists of the day to come see for themselves. They came, they saw, they believed. That's what you should have done."

James stood by the car, his thin chest heaving with the force of his breathing, and his eyes desperate. "What about the projectile points and the scraper? Armijo was there when I uncovered those. And David saw them, too."

Dr. Hagan seemed to freeze and ponderously turned to David. "When was this, and why didn't you tell me?"

"But I just thought we were s—supposed to . . . " he stuttered to a halt as he stared in puzzlement at the professor.

"When? Come on, son, get your thinking cap on.

100

When did you find them, and were the points Folsom or something else? Speak up, damn it!"

David flinched at the sharp sound of Hagan's voice, then he seemed to freeze. "Do you mean . . . ?" he started. At Dr. Hagan's nod, he closed his eyes and shook his head. "God, I don't believe it."

"Speak!" roared the professor.

Bob James grabbed Dr. Hagan's coat sleeve. "See, that's what you get for not taking this dig seriously. You were off visiting the Skin People when you should've been paying attention. We found them late Friday, but you can't blame David and me for not telling you. God, what with Armijo and Raul getting into it at supper, and the murder, and you running back to Albuquerque, we didn't have a chance." Bob James seemed to be enjoying the doctor's reaction.

"David?" asked Hagan.

"They were Folsom points," replied David.

"Photographs! Did you get photographs?"

The young assistant appeared dazed. "No, of course not. I mean I didn't have any film. Do I need photographs now?"

"Damn it to hell. You should have left the whole thing *in situ,* taken pictures, then packed the whole damn matrix up and sent it to the University. Let's get going. James, we'll stop by the hotel and get your camera; we can't be without a camera again. You do have a camera, don't you?" he asked sharply.

"Well, yes," answered Bob James, scratching his head.

"Good! Too bad it's not video. By God, I'll have one sent up from Albuquerque. Got to stay with the times. Projectile points and a scraper. Some digs don't yield that much in three seasons."

Charles wouldn't have believed someone as short and round as Dr. Hagan could move so fast. The professor's legs were almost a blur as he churned back across the road. "Come on, Bob, damn it! Let's get back to that dig."

"What about those crazies?" demanded Bob James.

Dr. Hagan had already climbed in the jeep. "Don't you worry about the Leader; I can handle him. Quit standing there; we've got a lot of digging to do and damn little decent weather left."

"I'm coming," shouted James, heading toward his jeep. "And we'll stop by the hotel for my shotgun just in case the Leader doesn't take to being handled."

Lindman stuck his head out of the car window. "You just leave that damn shotgun where it is, Bob James. I'm not having any more killing in my county." He rolled the window up and tapped Raul's shoulder. "Follow that jeep."

13

THE LEADER HIMSELF barred their way to the dig. He was an imposing figure, wearing a loincloth made of hide and a antelope-skin fur cloak with the tail still attached thrown about his shoulders. His moccasins, with high tops that covered half his calf, were stiff and crudely stitched. He carried an atl-atl in one hand, its darts and mainshaft were tucked in a quiverlike pouch slung over his shoulder. Charles had a hysterical urge to laugh; at least the atl-atl wasn't loaded.

He sobered instantly as he and Lindman got out of the car. The Leader wasn't the type to inspire laughter, or even to permit it. Gray-streaked hair brushed the tops of his shoulders, and his eyes were large and deep set under thick brows and of a brown so dark as to appear black. Those eyes dominated his face and, like Rasputin's, seemed to burn with an inner fire. Charles shivered and felt the fine hair at the nape of his neck prickle. The Leader's eyes were those of a man who'd visited hell and brought it back with him.

Lindman rested one hand on his gun. "Leader, this is Sheriff Matthews from Texas. He's a friend of Raul Trujillo, and he's my deputy. Now get your men out of Dr. Hagan's way, and come over here. Matthews has some interesting questions to ask, and you'd better have some answers or, so help me God, I'll make this county so hot, you'll have to pick up hides and atl-atls and leave."

The Leader, as tall as Charles's own six feet three, had

stared at Charles without blinking. Charles would have bet his life and not inconsiderable private income that the Leader already knew who he was.

Sweeping his cloak back over his shoulders, the Leader addressed Lindman, but his eyes never moved from Charles. "You must leave. The spirit of Folsom Man has been defiled. Murder was done on his shrine, and now you must not search out his secrets."

His words were an incantation, but Charles caught a false note. The Leader was good—he was very, very good—but he was an actor manipulating his audience; he lacked the fanatical belief in his own words.

Dr. Hagan came up, puffing like a steam engine from the exertion of walking up a slight incline to reach the dig. It didn't affect the volume of his voice or its authority. "Get these half-assed kids out of the way, or better yet, tell them to grab a trowel and get in the trench. We could have a major site on our hands. Damn it, Armijo found projectile points and a scraper."

"The hell he did," said Bob James, scrambling up the last few steps of the slope. "*I* found them. Armijo was standing around griping and writing in his notebook."

If Charles hadn't been watching closely, he would have missed the Leader's almost imperceptible catch of breath at Dr. Hagan's words. Strange that the man wasn't surprised by Charles's presence, but was shocked by the finding of artifacts at a dig.

"Dr. Hagan, you and Lessing and Bob can get on with your arrowhead hunting, but Matthews and me are going to have a little talk with the Leader and his band of merry men. And women," he added, in deference to the three females among the twelve or so scruffy-looking young men.

"In that case, we're commandeering Raul and your deputy," said Dr. Hagan firmly.

" 'Tonio?" said Lindman in ludicrous disbelief, then

shrugged his shoulders. "Go ahead; he's got to be good for something."

Hagan started issuing orders, and Charles decided the army had missed out on a great general or the Marines a drill sergeant. "David, you and Bob and Raul get back to the jeep and bring the extra equipment. Be damn careful with the camera."

"What do you want me to do, Dr. Hagan?" asked 'Tonio, standing at attention.

Hagan looked at the young man's swollen eye and evidently decided he wasn't to be trusted with carrying anything, included shovels. He patted 'Tonio's shoulder. "You just wait here by me, son. And don't salute," he added sharply when the deputy's arm made an upward motion.

The Leader jerked his head at his young followers and led the way to a large outcropping of lava. He sat down, and Charles's respect for the man went up a notch. Sitting on lava with its needle sharp texture while clad only in a loincloth called for a stoicism Charles knew he himself didn't possess.

The Leader's band crouched in a semicircle on the ground in front of him. They were a homogeneous group, Charles noticed; all were young, intelligent looking, dressed alike in leather pants and tunics. From the crackling sound when they moved and the stiff appearance of their garb, he concluded that Lindman was right: the Skin People couldn't tan leather worth a damn. And they definitely stank.

But there was something else. Like the Leader, there was a hint of play-acting about them. And while the three women weren't ugly, none qualified as a "looker." None looked to be the type to appeal to a man like Armijo.

Sheriff Lindman barged through the semicircle of bodies, propped one foot on the lava outcropping, and put his hands on his hips. "All right, Leader, tell me your story about your little excursion to Capulin the other night."

"I have told you."

"Tell me again. Matthews is real interested in hearing it."

The Leader glanced at Charles, then turned his head in the direction of the distant cinder cone. "We went to pay tribute to the spirit of Folsom Man, the great hunter who lived by strength and cunning in harmony with the land, worshipping his gods, one of which was fire."

Charles nodded. "And Capulin was your symbol of this god?"

"Capulin did not exist until three thousand years after Folsom Man hunted in this region. But it is still a fitting monument to him. Fire was a hunting weapon; he used it to stampede bison herds. And it was good hunting here. The climate was cooler and more moist, the grasses thicker and taller, the bison plentiful. We celebrated that with our chants in the very heart of a fire-giver."

"Did you know you had an audience for your performance?" asked Charles.

The Leader's eyelids flickered, and he inclined his head. "Certainly. When we found his body."

"You didn't hear or see anything that night? Armijo didn't cry out?" asked Charles, his eyes hard.

Something flashed in the Leader's eyes. "Armijo did not cry out. Those of us here did not know he had died until we were leaving the crater."

"Does that include Faith?" asked Lindman suddenly. "I notice she's not with you today."

"Faith is strong with feelings for the spirits. She is back at the cave recovering." The Leader's eyes were brooding.

A thud punctuated the Leader's statement. "Is she all right?" asked David Lessing anxiously.

Charles looked around. Lessing stood beside the ruck-sack he had dropped, with Bob James and Raul just behind him.

Lindman's black eyebrows came to within a fraction of an inch of colliding as he frowned at the interruption. "Get the hell into that ditch. When I need any help asking questions, I'll let Matthews here lend a hand." His frown deepened, and his eyebrows drew closer. "You heard me. Get out. Dr. Hagan, get these men out of earshot."

Hagan waved at them. "Into the trench, men; time's wasting." He turned and glared at Lindman. "You don't need to snap at the boy, Sheriff. He's not eavesdropping on anything important. We can all see that Faith's not in her usual place." He swung around and walked with ponderous dignity toward the trench.

Charles could practically hear Lindman grinding his teeth together as he sought to regain the momentum of his questioning. "So Faith is recovering from an experience with spirits. Does that mean she feels guilty about something? Is Armijo's ghost haunting her?" he demanded.

"She has nothing to be guilty about. She was with us that night; she could not have left the circle without being seen."

"You warned Armijo to stay away from her, but he didn't follow your orders, did he? Did you know she was meeting him at night in his room, that she climbed a tree beside the hotel and crawled through a window to be with him? Did you kill him for corrupting her? Or because she was more in his power than yours?"

The Leader didn't move, but Charles could see a pulse beating in his throat, and the knuckles on the hand that held the atl-atl were white. "If I had killed him, I would have done it more slowly." He said it with absolute conviction, and Charles believed him.

Lindman straightened up and glanced over at Charles with a look that said they were wasting their time. Charles agreed. The Leader was too intelligent to intimidate; he would repeat his story until the next ice age, and there was no way to break it without more evidence.

Questioning the little band of followers was equally futile. "We all walked to the crater and built the fire. The Leader started the chant and we joined in," said one redheaded young man who was scratching a rash. "We were to project ourselves backward in time and think and feel and react like Folsom Man." He grinned. "I bet Folsom Man wasn't allergic to animal fur."

"Did you see anyone on the slopes, or hear anything?" asked Charles.

"We were to keep our eyes focused on the fire; it aids in self-hypnosis. As for hearing anything, we were chanting. I might have heard a gunshot, but someone throwing an atl-atl, no."

"So you just sat like bumps staring at the fire and singing." Lindman was angry, disgusted, and frustrated.

The young man's wide-set blue eyes made him look angelic. "You don't understand how it is. It's a trance in a way, but nothing like a bad drug trip. It's letting your imagination free, it's a form of prayer . . . "

"Prayer! Father Mulholland would choke on his cigar if he heard that," muttered Lindman.

" . . . We use everything the Leader has taught us until we can feel the climate change, hear animal sounds from animals that are extinct."

"If they're extinct, how the hell you gonna know how they're supposed to sound?" asked Lindman, then flinched when Charles elbowed him in the ribs.

"We can feel the spirit of Folsom man, feel his fear of darkness, his desire for companionship." The young man stopped and scratched his chest. "That night—it's funny—I even thought I felt his *physical* presence—as though he was actually walking behind me. I guess you think I'm crazy?"

Lindman opened his mouth to answer, but Charles frowned at him. "So someone could have left the circle, and none of you might even remember it?"

"Yeah, I guess that's right," he replied with a grin. "If you're through with me, I want to go help with the dig. Maybe I'll find a skeleton." At Charles's nod, he rushed off toward the trench with an exuberant cry.

"Well, that's it," said Lindman. "The last of the nuts to interview, and he was the nuttiest one."

"Nobody saw or heard anything until they started back and stumbled over the body," mused Charles. "A trance, that kid said. Damn it, this is the strangest cult I've ever had any experience with. There's no evidence of drugs, no dilated pupils, bad skin tone, incoherent speech, no apparent nervousness. They could all be Boy Scouts playing Indians at a camp-out. What kind of power does the Leader have over them? Usually in a cult it's drugs, or the members are misfits and stay because they feel accepted. But these kids seem so normal," said Charles, beating a clenched fist against the palm of his other hand.

"Except they sleep in a cave and run around in rotten animal skins," said Lindman sourly. "Do you believe them?"

Charles nodded. "Yes, I believe they believe what they're saying. I think they were too busy playing Indian to notice what the chief was doing."

"What do you mean?"

"Do you believe the Leader was in a trance?"

Lindman snorted. "That guy gives trances; he doesn't get them."

"Let's rescue Raul and 'Tonio from Dr. Hagan. I want to interview Faith."

Lindman looked over toward the trench. The Leader's band had happily dispersed and, armed with tools of various shapes, including what looked like knives and awls, had joined the dig. "Why don't we leave them here? If we drag them off, the Leader's gonna know where we're going. Besides, unless I gag 'Tonio, he's liable to try to show off in front of Faith, and I'll end up kicking his butt. I ain't in the mood for that."

Charles grinned. He knew exactly what Lindman meant. There were days he'd taken Slim Fletcher along on an investigation and spent the whole time wishing he'd left him back in town. "Suit yourself, but I don't think we'll fool the Leader; he's too intelligent for that. Not that it matters, since we have a car and he doesn't. We'll get there before he can."

14

THE SKIN PEOPLE'S cave wasn't really a cave at all, but a twenty-five-foot basalt overhang. They had chipped out the hardened lava to deepen the area beneath it. The interior had been divided into three cubicles by means of wooden posts set in the ground, with hide strung between them. The two smaller cubicles, filled with pallets of grasses covered by the inevitable hides, were on either end of the interior, separated by a large common room. Evidently the Leader didn't believe in communal sleeping, because the living arrangements reminded Charles of a dormitory.

They found Faith huddled in the corner of one of the sleeping cubicles. "Faith, it's Sheriff Lindman. We need to talk to you."

The girl hid her face behind crossed arms until only the top of her head was visible. "No, please," came a muffled voice.

Lindman reached out awkwardly to pat the girl's shoulder, but Faith shrank back until she sat with her back to the wall. Lindman pulled his hand back and stared perplexedly at her. "I'm not going to hurt you, Faith," he said in the tone of voice he'd use with a frightened child. "This is Mr. Matthews. He's Raul's friend and came all the way from Texas to help him."

"He brought me wildflowers one day to put in the cave," said Faith unexpectedly as she lowered her arms and looked up at them.

Charles quite literally caught his breath. Faith just

missed being the most beautiful woman he'd ever seen. She was a natural blonde, unusual in itself, but her features were perfect: oval face, delicately shaped brows, large blue eyes, aristocratic nose, wide full mouth, long graceful neck. She was like a beautiful cameo that someone had smudged with dirty fingers. Her gilt hair, although clean, lacked luster; her skin was mottled; and her blue eyes were marred with broken veins and an expression of hopelessness beyond anything in his experience. He felt pity twist his belly into knots.

He swallowed and prayed his voice didn't sound too thick. "Raul is a nice man, isn't he?" At her tiny nod he continued. "Did you know he's in trouble?" She stiffened, then nodded again. "Can you help him? Can you tell us about the night at Capulin? You left the circle, didn't you? One of the followers said he felt the presence of Folsom Man behind him, seeking companionship. But it wasn't Folsom Man, was it? It was you as you rejoined the circle."

She pulled the pelt higher until only her thin fingers with their bitten nails and her face showed above it. "Please," she whimpered.

"Please what, Faith? Please don't ask you, or please don't make you tell? I have to, because Raul is innocent; he wouldn't hurt anyone."

Her face twisted and aged with lines of bitterness. "You can't be sure; you can't ever be sure," she cried.

Charles's own doubts surfaced. "No, but I can trust. That's really all we can ever do, isn't it?"

She searched his face, and he watched the hopelessness deepen in her eyes. "You're pretending, too, just like everybody else," she said.

Her accusation seemed to burrow its way through his defenses. "No!"

She smiled, if such a grimace could be termed a smile. "Who taught you not to trust?"

He's dead, thought Charles wildly. *L.D. Lassiter is dead, but I can still trust. If I can't, I'm no better than this hopeless girl.* "Just tell me what happened. Help Raul."

She clutched the pelt tighter, twisting her fingers restlessly. Her blank expression changed to desperation. "I can't help him. Please don't try to make me."

Charles grasped her wrists. "Why?" he cried desperately. "Did you see him murder Enrique? Is that it? Or was it somebody else? Somebody you're trying to protect?"

"Let her go!" commanded a voice, and strong arms circled his neck and pulled, sending him sprawling across the floor. But not before he'd seen the double track of needle marks on the inside of Faith's arms.

"That's enough," shouted Lindman, rising to a crouch and pulling his gun. "Back off, Leader! Right now," he added as he pulled the hammer back on his revolver, and the click of the cylinder announced the positioning of a shell.

Faith screamed, and scrambling to her feet, ran out of the cave.

The Leader stood over Charles, his face flushed from rage, his eyes burning like coals. "Leave her alone or I'll kill you!"

Charles pushed himself to a seated position and leaned back against the basalt wall. Its texture was rough against his back, but he barely felt it. "Like you killed Armijo?" he asked, exhausted.

"His own evil killed him. He dared to defile sacred knowledge, to steal what was not his. And he paid the price."

"Stuff the mysticism," said Lindman crudely. "We're talking about a murder, and I'm not gonna argue the point of whether he deserved it or not. But nobody"— he stabbed the Leader's chest with the barrel of his gun—"*nobody* makes that decision in my county. Now we're going after that girl and taking her back to town."

The Leader folded his arms. "You will accomplish nothing; she will not speak."

Pushing himself to his feet, Charles grabbed the Leader's robe, jerking him to within a few inches of his own body. "You damn fool! Don't you understand? If she knows something, if she saw the killer that night, then he might also have seen her. She must tell us what she knows for her own sake; she won't be safe otherwise."

The Leader blinked, but not before Charles saw a flash of hesitation in those burning eyes so close to his own. "She will go back to the dig. She will be safe."

Charles shoved him away. "No, she won't. All the suspects are there. Except you," he added.

There was a pause before the Leader answered. "Dr. Hagan is her friend. And David Lessing."

"But neither one of them has an alibi for the murder."

"Even if they were guilty, they wouldn't kill Faith." He sounded totally convinced.

Charles was getting tired of witnesses being so sure of themselves about one thing or another.

"You're a fool if you believe that. Only the first murder is hard, the second and third are easier. By the fourth, the murderer thinks no more of killing than he would of swatting flies. It's a progressive illness that's only terminal to other people. Will you risk her life on trusting a man who's already committed that first murder? Whatever his motive, if he's willing to frame Raul to protect himself, then what do you think he would do to a girl who's a real danger to him?"

The Leader's conviction shattered, and he turned to stagger toward the cave entrance and Bob James's jeep.

Lindman pushed Charles toward the jeep. "Go with him. I'll go over to the hotel and call the office to get the state police out here, in case we have to search for her.

114

I've only got three deputies and that's not enough. I'll catch up with you in a few minutes."

"A few minutes?"

Lindman pointed to the south. "Hotel's just about three miles away. Now get going before that crazy man runs off and leaves you."

Charles ran for the jeep.

The Leader gunned the engine, swung the jeep in a circle, and turned down the narrow asphalt road back toward the dig. He pointed out of the window on Charles's side. "Keep watching for her. That ridge is the beginning of Johnson Mesa, but the underbrush is the best cover until we reach the turnoff for the dig. I want to get there ahead of her."

"Why?" demanded Charles bitterly. "So you can protect her, or shut her up?"

The Leader didn't answer, and the silence continued until they drove up to the dig and stopped, stirring up a swirl of dust.

Dr. Hagan's head popped out of the trench first, like a jack-in-the-box, followed by the rest of him. *It's like watching a block of granite defy gravity,* thought Charles as Hagan rushed toward the car, his stocky legs churning up dust and bits of dead grass. "Why did you take the car, you idiot? Never mind, I don't have time to listen. Matthews, turn that jeep around and head back toward the hotel. You," he said, pointing a stubby finger at the Leader, "get out of there and come look. We need you as a witness until we can call in other archeologists. Don't sit there staring at me! Get out!"

"Faith has run away," said the Leader.

Dr. Hagan waved a hand. "We'll look for her later. She can't get far in this country. This is more important."

"What are you talking about, Dr. Hagan?" demanded Charles.

"Lindman's deputy—"

" 'Tonio?" asked Charles with a sinking feeling.

"If that's his name. Anyway, he was climbing out of the trench and grabbed an exposed rock for a handhold. The rock came loose and started a small landslide. Bob James was all for conducting an experiment on the efficiency of flint knives at butchering, with 'Tonio playing the part of the bison, but one of your kids, the redheaded one that's always scratching, yelled out that he could see a part of a skull. Everybody rushed over, and we excavated a little more and, by God, he was right!"

The Leader jumped down from the jeep and grasped Dr. Hagan by the lapels. "Don't you understand? Faith is out there somewhere with no one to protect her."

Dr. Hagan pushed away the Leader's hands and straightened his shirt. "She'll be all right. Bob James, David, and Raul are cutting across country toward the hotel to start making calls and to round up some more equipment. If they run into her, they'll take care of her. By the way, Bob James was screaming like a newly branded calf about your stealing his jeep."

"Damn it, Dr. Hagan, those men are all suspects," yelled Charles as he awkwardly climbed over the gear shift into the driver's seat of the jeep.

The Leader pulled himself into the passenger's seat. "Go!" he said tersely and Charles gunned the jeep into a tight circle.

Dr. Hagan grabbed hold as the jeep skidded by and tipped himself head first into the back seat. A series of "oofs" and "uhs," followed by some imaginative oaths, issued from the professor before he managed to right himself. "Now what's this all about?" he demanded, wiping a smudge of dirt from the end of his nose.

"Faith left the circle that night," admitted the Leader. "She saw something or someone."

116

"Who?" asked the professor sharply.

"We don't know," said Charles. "She wouldn't tell us, she just ran."

"So you still don't know," said Dr. Hagan slowly.

"Damn it," said Charles. "Why did she run away? Doesn't she realize she's in danger?"

"If you were a frightened young girl, would you be anxious to point the finger at someone capable of murdering a man, particularly someone who had stalked his victim like a Folsom Man tracking a bison? I think you're asking too much. Faith's first reaction would be to deny it, then, if confronted by authority in the persons of two sheriffs, to hide. Or perhaps she was . . . " The professor stopped abruptly.

"Was what, Dr. Hagan?" asked Charles, glancing in the rear view mirror and frowning. The professor had his eyes closed and his blunt features looked as if they were sculptured in sand and ready to crumble.

"Protecting someone," he whispered.

"Who?" Charles waited, then slammed on the brakes and turned to stare at the professor. "Damn it, who?"

Dr. Hagan's usual booming voice was a hushed, funeral sound. "David Lessing."

"Damn it, how long have you suspected him? Were you going to let Raul spend the rest of his life in prison, or were you planning to keep quiet until Lessing had a chance to disappear?"

"I didn't say David was guilty; I said Faith may have been protecting him." Dr. Hagan's voice was a bellow of indignation.

"Please, drive," said the Leader. "You can ask your questions later."

Charles turned around and stepped on the accelerator. *First find Faith, then get some answers.*

Lindman came roaring toward them in Charles's car, as Charles braked to a stop. He swerved to avoid hitting them, bumped over several clumps of dry grass, and finally came to a stop a few feet from a lava squeeze-up. He piled out of the car and vaulted into the back of the jeep beside Dr. Hagan. "What's wrong? Why are you heading this way? I thought you were so damn sure she'd go to the dig."

"Bob James, Lessing, and Raul went back to the hotel. They're between her and the dig," explained Charles.

"How far ahead are they?" asked Lindman, turning to Dr. Hagan.

"The, er, Leader's dust had hardly settled when they left. Say thirty minutes or more. And David is a runner. And Bob James and Raul were keeping up with him, at least at the beginning."

Charles turned the wheel viciously to the right off the faint road that had been made by the daily treks to the dig. He fought to control the jeep as it bounced over the rough terrain. A steady stream of curses in English, Spanish, and Norwegian came from Lindman as he fought to keep from being thrown out. Dr. Hagan, with his rotund body rolling from side to side, uttered an "oof" each time he jostled Lindman.

Charles stepped on the brake, sending the jeep into a spin, slammed the clutch into reverse, and backed away from a deep ravine. The Leader vaulted out of the jeep, followed by Dr. Hagan.

Lindman picked himself off the floorboard and climbed out of the back seat. "I thought you were going to kill us, you damn fool."

Charles ignored him, intent only on finding the terrified young girl whose disturbed mind held the only evidence that would free Raul. Or might not. But he didn't dare let himself consider that.

He scrambled down the ravine and up the other side ahead of Lindman. "Wait!" he shouted, but the Leader had already disappeared. Dr. Hagan, moving faster than

Charles believed possible, waddled into the underbrush and vanished from sight. Charles looked across the empty countryside, where a hundred girls could hide in its ravines, bushes, and boulders. And so could a murderer.

"We've got to catch up to them," gasped Charles as he stumbled toward the spot where Dr. Hagan had disappeared and hoped it was also the Leader's vanishing point.

Lindman was cursing between panting breaths. "Damn boots! I'm sliding all over everywhere."

"Shut up and run," snapped Charles, then added some profanity of his own as he stepped on a tiny rock hidden in the dead grass and fell, sprawling.

Lindman reached down to help him up, but Charles pushed his hand away. "Go on; we've got to find her. We can't trust any of them."

"Not even Raul?" asked Lindman, hauling Charles to his feet in spite of his protests.

Charles started running again, blood dripping from a gash in his thigh. Hot spasms of pain shot through his leg to join the ones in his belly. What if Faith had meant she couldn't help Raul because he was guilty, not because she was protecting someone else?

He and Lindman burst through a screen of scrubby pine. "Raul!" he yelled as he headed toward the figure crouched beneath an outcropping of lava.

Raul looked up, then rose and stood with head bowed. He stretched out his right hand and unfolding his fingers, revealed a flint skinning-knife. Charles fell to his knees and vomited helplessly, but the image of bright red blood staining Raul's palm would not fade.

Lindman knelt and squeezed his shoulder. "Go on back, Sheriff; I'll take care of it from here."

And Charles walked back toward the jeep, never knowing that, like the Leader, his eyes were now those of a man who had visited hell.

15

CHARLES CLIMBED STIFFLY out of the jeep and absently dropped the key into his coat pocket. His fingers touched the two speeding tickets issued in New Mexico and the one issued in Texas. He must remember to pay them. But he'd worry about that tomorrow. Today he needed comfort, and warmth, and to be cared for.

Stepping upon the porch of the sprawling old red brick house, with its white trim beginning to peel, he rang the door bell.

"Charles." Angie's voice sounded breathless. The light from the hall silhouetted her in the doorway, leaving her face in shadow.

He did none of the things he told himself he'd do. He didn't explain why he was there. He didn't even wait to be invited in. He simply walked in, closed the door, and enfolded her in his arms. He rested his cheek against the top of her head and closed his eyes. "I need you, Angie."

Showered, shaved, dressed in clean clothes Meenie had brought over, and replete with a beef casserole Angie had practically forced him to eat, he felt better physically. Emotionally he felt as if he might shatter. He'd tried to talk to Meenie while he shaved, but his scrawny ex-cowboy deputy had shaken his head. "I figure if you'd wanted my help after that girl was killed in New Mexico, you'd be standin' in *my* bathroom lookin' like something that's been dragged behind a horse instead of here in Mrs. Lassiter's. But you ain't, and the lady who owns this bathroom is makin' you somethin' to eat and cryin' because she's afraid you're gonna change your mind and not let her fix whatever's ailin' you. So I'm not gonna listen to you, and Miss Poole ain't either or anybody else in the sheriff's department. Besides, Mrs. Lassiter ain't got a spittoon and I'm needin' one. See you later, Sheriff," he said and left Charles standing in the middle of Angie's bathroom.

"Charles?" Angie's hesitant voice pulled him back to the present, and he could feel her hand tremble. "I don't mean to push you. I just wanted you to know I'll listen if you want to tell me about it."

He looked at her and felt something snap into place in his mind. He knew why he had needed Raul to be innocent, and it had very little to do with belief in his deputy's character. In freeing Raul, he would be freeing himself. One friend had betrayed his trust by lying and murdering; another friend must cancel out that betrayal by being truthful and innocent. He needed Raul to restore the ability to trust that L.D. Lassiter had destroyed. For that was the source of his stubborn insistence that Angie not be told the truth about L.D. He simply hadn't trusted her enough to risk it. Meenie was right; he was afraid she'd think him a murderer.

But Raul wasn't innocent; therefore, he must restore himself. Otherwise he'd become as emotionally crippled as Faith had been, and his doubt would extend to himself and turn into self-hate just as hers had. Something within him recognized the danger and sent him back to the one person he loved more than he distrusted. And he discovered love was stronger than guilt or doubt or mistrust.

Charles swung his feet off the couch and sat up. He took Angie's hand and held it between his. "You're not pushing me, Angie, although maybe you should have told me off before yesterday." He stopped and took a deep breath, like a swimmer before going underwater. "Hang on, love, because it's a long story."

He started off by telling her about Faith's death, about the terrible tableau of Raul crouching over the girl's body with a knife. But he made himself go back to his other nightmare—the death of her husband, L.D.

He felt her hand tighten around his until her fingers were white as he told her that her dead husband was a murderer. He faltered as he came to his part in the conspiracy to cover up L.D.'s own murder. "L.D.'s plane didn't accidently crash, Angie; it was shot down."

Her face was completely white and her hazel eyes looked wounded. "Did you do it, Charles?"

He swallowed. "No, but I might as well have. I made the decision not to arrest the man who did. That makes me an accessory to L.D.'s murder."

"Who killed L.D., Charles?"

"A relative of one of his victims. I'd rather not say who. This is my confession, and I don't want to drag anyone else into it."

She sat looking down at their clasped hands until he couldn't stand it any longer. "Angie." He cleared his throat. "What are you thinking?"

She glanced up and his breath caught. The forlorn shadows that had haunted her eyes were gone, replaced by an expression of serenity and peace. "I'm glad you didn't kill him. Not that it would've changed my feelings for you, but because you would've never forgiven yourself." She smiled at him. "You're shocked, aren't you?"

He felt off-balance, like a drunk trying to walk a straight line. "You didn't hear what I said. I let his murderer go; that's the same thing as killing him myself."

She laid her hand against his cheek. "No, it isn't; you committed an act of mercy. Why punish a man who shoots a mad dog? And L.D. was worse than a mad dog because he knew what he was doing."

122

"Angie! He was your husband!"

She nodded her head. "And I cried for him, and even that was a gift from you. If you had arrested his killer, I would've been crying for my daughters. For the rest of their lives, they'd would've lived with knowing their father was a murderer. That wouldn't have been justice, Charles. They didn't pick L.D. for their father; I did. Why should they pay for my mistake?"

She looked at his shocked face, and he watched the tears begin to fill her eyes. "You think I'm hard, don't you, Charles? You expected me to cry, didn't you? Well, I think I'm going to, but not for L.D. I'm crying for you because you lied to protect me, and you're too decent to have to lie, and I can't even have hysterics like you think I should"—she wiped her eyes with the back of her hand—"because I don't think it's wrong to hate what L.D. was."

Charles moved without thinking, gathering her into his arms and settling her in his lap. He didn't remember later all the things he whispered to her, but he vividly remembered when his need to comfort her became a much more basic need. Because that's when the phone rang.

"Let it ring," he whispered between kisses.

"I can't. The girls are at the ranch with Dad. Something may have happened." Her voice sounded breathless.

"Damn!" he said as he sat up and watched her scramble to the phone.

While Angie answered the phone he tried to regain control of his libido. He might as well have tried to stop a rampaging bull. He vaulted off the couch and over to her just as she picked up the phone.

"Hello," she said and caught her breath in an audible gasp as Charles kissed the hollow of her throat, then began nibbling his way to more interesting territory.

Angie dropped the phone as she leaned back in his arms to allow him unrestricted territorial exploration, but Charles could still hear the Norwegian accent of the caller. "Hello! Hello! Is anybody there?"

Charles lifted his mouth just shy of his target, grabbed the dangling receiver, and yelled into it. "Damn it, Lindman, how did you get this number?"

"Meenie Higgins decided he didn't want me swearing out a warrant for your arrest for transporting a stolen vehicle across state lines."

Charles released Angie and leaned against the wall, nausea making his face greasy with perspiration, as the horror he'd left a few hours ago overwhelmed him. "What do you want, Lindman? To say you told me so, that if I'd stayed out of the investigation, Raul would still be in jail and Faith would be alive? Consider it said."

"In case nobody's ever told you, you're not Christ, and you ought to stop carrying the guilt of the world around on your shoulders. Now climb back in Bob James's jeep and get your butt back to New Mexico. Polanski's back from Albuquerque with the answers to that list of questions you sent with him. You started this whole mess, and you're gonna help me finish it."

Charles gripped the receiver until his knuckles turned white. "Do you mean Raul's not guilty?"

"I mean I'm not sure. Hell, I'm not even sure of my own name. You just get back here. The state police'll meet you at Texline and escort you to Clayton. Can't have you getting any more tickets."

"Texline is in Texas!" yelped Charles. "The New Mexico State Police don't have any jurisdiction in Texas!"

There was a tired chuckle from the other end of the line. "They don't? You tell them that when you get to Texline," Lindman said and hung up.

Charles replaced the receiver and started to button his shirt. "I have to go back to Clayton," he said to Angie, feeling awkward and embarrassed. What should he say to her? He couldn't just say thanks for dinner and leave, not after telling her L.D. had been a murderer and then mauling her on her own couch.

He cleared his throat. "Angie, about what happened . . ."

"You mean when you almost made love to me? "Don't you dare apologize, Charles."

His mouth dropped open, and he stuttered. "B—but it was the wrong time. After hearing about L.D., you were in no condition to make love with another man. You were in shock," he finished weakly.

She shook her head and rose on tiptoes to kiss him. "Charles, you're such a nice man, but sometimes you're so blind. Did I act like I was in shock? Did I even act surprised?"

Charles felt dizzy and clutched her shoulders for support. "What are you saying?"

She smoothed her fingers over his chest, an action that did nothing to calm him. "I'm telling you, Charles, that I always suspected L.D. had something to do with the murders."

"That's impossible!" exclaimed Charles.

She raised an eyebrow. "Is it? I knew L.D. better than anyone, and I didn't believe he'd just leave. He had too much to lose. His political career for one thing; he wouldn't just walk off and leave that, not as long as he thought he could talk or charm his way out of whatever mess he was in. Then L.D.'s secretary told me that you, Meenie, and Raul were all looking for him that day. I didn't think you were looking for him just to say good-bye, particularly Meenie. He wouldn't have walked across the street to say good-bye to L.D., much less go to the airport. Then the insurance claim on L.D.'s plane was

125

disallowed because pieces were missing from the wreck and the FAA couldn't reconstruct exactly what had happened. You and Meenie and Raul stood guard over the wreck. Only one of you could have removed part of it. After that, it was simple. You tried to stop L.D. from leaving, and in the process he was killed. You wouldn't try to stop him unless a crime was involved, and there was only one crime you were investigating: the murders of Maria Martinez and Billy Joe Williams."

"Why didn't you tell me?" he demanded, grasping her shoulders and holding her away from him.

"Because you had to trust me enough to tell me yourself," she answered, smiling at his astonished expression.

He pulled her into his arms again, tilting her chin up with one hand. "Did I ever fool you about anything?"

She looked thoughtful for a second. "Yes. I never was sure about how you felt about me."

"Are you sure now?" he asked, his voice so husky he hardly recognized it.

She nodded, and an interval followed that threatened the self-control he'd managed to regain. Finally he lifted his head toward the ceiling and sucked in several deep breaths. "I have to go, Angie."

"To help Raul?" she asked, stepping away from him and watching the customary sternness settle over his features like a mask.

He nodded. "And to apologize for doubting him." He gathered his coat and Stetson, and left.

Angie closed the door behind him and leaned her forehead against the smooth wood. It was finally over. L.D.'s lingering presence was gone, and Charles was free.

16

THE JEEP CIRCLED the old tin-roofed courthouse and skidded into the parking lot. The lights were on in the old jailer's building, which now housed the Union County sheriff's office. Charles vaulted out of the jeep, waved his thanks to the New Mexico state police officers who'd met him in Texline, and banged through the screen door into Lindman's office.

Lindman glanced up from his desk, his eyes looking like red-streaked blue marbles. "You sure as hell look pleased about something. Enjoy your trip back to the Lone Star state?"

"It was . . . enlightening," he said as he stepped across the room toward where Raul sat in one of the armless chairs, resting his handcuffed wrists on his knees.

"Raul, I'm sorry," Charles said, thinking how inadequate his words were.

Raul looked up, and Charles stifled a gasp. His deputy's eyes were sunken, red-rimmed, and feverish-looking. The stubble of beard on his face was longer, darker, and seemed to emphasize the grooves of fatigue around his mouth. His normally swarthy skin was sallow, and he looked sick and hopeless.

Raul licked his lips, and Charles noticed they looked cracked and dry. "When you saw me, you looked as if you'd seen a ghost, Sheriff."

Charles had, but he had no intention of telling Raul that he'd compared him to L.D. He'd already indulged himself in one confession tonight; that was enough. "Tell me what happened."

Raul shook his head and lifted his hands in the start of one his eloquent Latin gestures. The handcuffs rattled, and he let his hands fall in self-defeat. "The girl came running toward me . . . "

"With a knife in her back?" Lindman stood over them, hands on hips.

Raul flushed and resolutely kept his eyes on Charles. "She came around that boulder . . . "

"Lava squeeze-up," interjected Polanski, then backed up a step when Charles looked at him. "Didn't mean to interrupt," he said apologetically.

"Go on, Raul," urged Charles.

Raul lifted his hands and wiped the sweat off his forehead. "She had her hands behind her back, trying to pull out the knife. She fell, and I pulled out the knife. I was going to use my shirt to make a compress to stop the bleeding, but then you drove up. I didn't kill her, Sheriff," he whispered.

"Where'd the knife come from, Lindman?" asked Charles without taking his eyes off Raul.

"From the dig. It belonged to one of the Leader's kids. He laid it down, and the next thing he knew it was gone. Of course, anybody could've taken it," Lindman added.

Raul looked at Charles, confused, frightened, and desperate to understand. "I don't know why all this is happening to me."

"You were an opportunity, Raul, that's all. You were in the wrong place at the wrong time." He rubbed his thigh, now cleaned, disinfected, bandaged, and aching badly. "Now, where were Lessing and Bob James?"

"I don't know. I'd twisted my ankle." He smiled wryly and lifted one leg. "Boots are not good to run in."

"You didn't see Bob James or Lessing ahead of you?" asked Charles.

Raul shook his head. "I didn't see anybody."

"The Leader? Dr. Hagan? They couldn't have been very far away. Didn't they pass you?"

"I heard some crashing in the undergrowth, but I couldn't see anything. I thought maybe it was Lessing or James coming back to see what had happened to me. I called out, but nobody answered."

"The Leader and Dr. Hagan showed up just about the time you took off," said Lindman.

"Together?" asked Charles sharply.

"No," answered Lindman, shaking his head. "The Leader was first, then Hagan."

Charles got to his feet. "If I'd been faster, or hadn't fallen, or if you hadn't stopped to help me up, we'd have been there in time." He leaned over Raul, his voice a frustrated snarl. "Why the hell were you going back to the hotel? Why couldn't you have stayed at the dig where twelve or fourteen people could testify for you?"

Raul closed his eyes. "I wanted to call my wife," he answered flatly.

Polanski looked completely bewildered. "You could have called your wife anytime."

Raul straightened, his brown eyes beginning to sparkle with the first expression besides defeat that Charles had seen since coming to New Mexico. "I am a deputy sheriff. I have always been a deputy sheriff, since I was a very young man. But here, I am a suspect. To be around those people at the dig, to be looked at, to know some of them think I am a murderer . . . " His voice broke, and he drew a breath. "I am *not* a murderer, and I needed to talk to someone who believed me."

"I understand, Raul," said Charles, uncomfortably aware that he also had thought Raul guilty. "Is there nothing else you can tell us?"

His deputy shook his head, and Charles turned to Polanski. "Let's see your reports from Albuquerque."

Polanski cleared his throat, blew his nose, and withdrew some papers from his briefcase. "I found out some very interesting information and, if we didn't keep finding Mr. Trujillo in compromising positions, I would say we had a very good case against at least two other people."

Whatever he discovered in Albuquerque must have shaken him badly, thought Charles as he sat down at Lindman's desk, propped his feet on its top, and started reading.

After several minutes, he dimly smelled coffee and nodded his thanks without looking up when a cup appeared at his elbow. When he finished the last page, he laid it face down on the stack of other papers and carefully aligned the edges, squinting as he did so. "Have you read all this, Lindman?"

"Yes, and I'm with Polanski. If Raul didn't keep getting in the way, we might be able to catch ourselves a killer."

"Then you agree that all these reports reveal an elaborate conspiracy to commit murder?" asked Charles, tapping the stack of papers.

Lindman sank down in a chair and scratched his head. "I don't know that I'd say 'elaborate conspiracy,' Matthews; those are strong words. It may just be coincidence that all three of the people involved with Linda Denise Oberman's suicide were in Folsom at the same time. Armijo was the University's expert on Folsom Man, and Hagan was Chairman of the Archeology Department, so naturally he'd be at the site sometimes. As for Lessing, he might not have been in touch with Armijo at all until a little while ago. Bob James did say it was a month or more before Armijo made an appearance."

Charles's fist came down on the desk with a thud that jerked Lindman upright on his chair. "Maybe you ought to read the police report again on"—he consulted a zeroxed page—"the Oberman suicide. David Lessing, described as her fiancé, found her body. Dr. William Alfred Hagan, close friend of the family, made quite a nuisance of himself by claiming Miss Oberman was murdered. Dr. Enrique Armijo was the last person to see Miss Oberman alive, and he states she was hysterical, depressed, and abusive toward him personally." He looked up at Lindman.

"You've been a prosecutor, you know the D.A. isn't going to court and try to prove something like a conspiracy to murder Armijo with nothing to go on but that. They'd just stand pat on their stories and scream coincidence. Their defense attorney would get the case thrown out of court, then sue this county for false arrest. Hell, the county can hardly afford liability insurance now. Can you imagine how much premiums would go up if we lost a lawsuit?"

Charles's boots hit the floor, and he rose to his feet. "Do you believe Raul killed Enrique Armijo?"

Lindman closed his eyes. "No," he admitted.

"Do you believe he killed Faith?"

The sheriff's eyes snapped open. "Damn it, Matthews, that's the problem. If he didn't kill Armijo, why should he kill Faith? But we found him with blood on his hands." He shook his head. "I can't believe he's innocent of one murder without believing he's innocent of the other. But I do, and that's impossible."

Charles took two steps and helped Raul up. He watched him gingerly stand on one foot and use the other only for balance.

"Sit down, Raul," said Charles, grasping his arm and helping him back onto the chair. "Sheriff Lindman, Inspector Polanski." He clasped his hands together behind his back and started to pace. "When I first got here, I thought the whole case sounded like something out of *Alice in Wonderland*: murder weapons disappearing, the victim turning up in what you might say resembles the world's biggest rabbit hole, a group of suspects more eccentric than the guests at the Mad Hatter's tea party. I don't want to push that analogy too far, but like the book, we are asked to keep believing impossible things, the first being that Raul is guilty."

"I don't understand how that's so impossible," said Polanski.

"Because Raul has no place in this particular little fantasy. He's the only participant who isn't interested in archeology. And he doesn't have a motive to murder Faith."

Lindman stiffened up like a bird dog who just sighted an elusive quarry. "What the hell are you talking about, Matthews? Of course he had a motive. She was a witness to Armijo's murder."

"You said it yourself. If he's guilty, why bother to kill Faith? You already have an airtight case against him. He has motive, opportunity, and has been caught with the weapon. And there's another thing. Which direction was her body pointing, Lindman?"

"West, toward the dig," answered the sheriff, his eyes narrowed as he tried to follow Charles's reasoning.

Charles expelled a breath of relief. If Lindman had answered differently, he would have blown an irreparable hole in Raul's defense. "And Raul was going east, away from the dig. In other words, she was running toward Raul, a man she was supposedly terrified of."

Polanski interrupted. "Perhaps she didn't know he was there; perhaps she ran into him by accident."

"Raul called out; she knew who she was running toward. She was running toward the only safe person, the only outsider, the only one not involved in whatever was going on at that dig. And look at it from another angle. She would have had to run past him, then stop to allow him to stab her in the back, because he certainly couldn't have chased her with a twisted ankle. That's another impossible thing we're being asked to believe. What did happen? How was this little scene set up? Think back, Lindman. Everyone was standing around when the Leader made his statement about Faith and the spirits. Hagan, Raul, Lessing, and Bob James were all listening. And looking."

"What does looking have to do with anything?" demanded Lindman.

"Maybe the murderer didn't realize that Faith wasn't in the circle at Capulin until he saw the same circle without her again, with everybody making a point of the fact she wasn't there. It's like one of those party games where you're asked to look at a picture or a group of objects, then make a list of everything you can remember seeing. Sometimes you can swear you've listed everything—until you see the same picture or objects again to check against your list. We provided the murderer with another chance to check his memory. Once we did that, the murderer took the first opportunity to leave the dig. Suppose instead of heading for the hotel, he headed for the cave. On the way, he meets Faith, grabs her, waits until he sees Raul, then stabs her and pushes her right into Raul's path, depending on Raul's helping her and incriminating himself further."

"Then it's either Bob James or David Lessing." said Lindman, rubbing his chin as if debating which one was most likely.

Charles ran his fingers through his hair. "Not necessarily. It might have been the Leader. Maybe he wanted to get to the dig first so he could stop her from talking to anyone. When he found the others were gone, he seized the opportunity to follow, depending on his greater familiarity with the terrain to help him find her. And Dr. Hagan was out of everybody's sight."

"Do you really suspect that old man?" demanded Lindman.

"He's lied to us, not once but several times. I don't trust him any more than I do anyone else, and that means not at all."

Polanski was nodding his head. "All of your scenarios are entirely possible, Sheriff Matthews, and quite logical. Unfortunately, I don't see how any of them can be proved."

Charles stopped his pacing. Polanski was right; it couldn't be proved. It was all negative evidence: it didn't prove Raul was guilty, but it didn't prove he wasn't either. Everything was ambiguous, everything but the atl-atl.

He whirled around and grabbed Raul. "When did you last look in that closet before Sunday morning when Sheriff Lindman searched it?" He shook Raul. "Think, damn it!"

"Saturday night! I got my bathrobe and some clean clothes for Sunday."

"And then what?" demanded Charles. "What did you do next?"

"I went to shower. Sheriff Lindman had questioned me several times that day, and I felt dirty."

"You walked down the hall to the bathroom, and someone slipped into your room and hid a bloody atl-atl in your closet?"

"Yes! No! I don't know! Sheriff Lindman told me the atl-atl was in the back of the closet, behind some clothes of Mrs. James's. I might not have noticed it." He buried his face in his hands. The handcuffs rattled with his movement.

"I know when it wasn't there" said Charles firmly.

"When?" Lindman's voice cracked like a whip.

"The night of the murder. Remember Raul's statement? He stated he was in bed by midnight. The pathologist estimates the time of death at one o'clock, more or less. The killer had to hide the atl-atl somewhere else until he had an opportunity to put it in Raul's closet."

"That's presupposing we believe Raul's statement," said Polanski.

Charles and Lindman ignored Polanski. "So where was it?" asked Lindman.

"I don't know, but I'm betting it was in the hotel. Let's get a search warrant and see if we can find any evidence of where it might have been hidden. You said it still had blood on it Sunday morning?" At Lindman's nod, Charles continued. "When it was hidden Friday night, that blood was fresh. And fresh blood will smear on anything it touches. Can we get a lab team up here, Lindman?"

Lindman grabbed the phone. "Damn right we can. The criminal investigation lab in Santa Fe will fly a team in."

Charles felt a trickle of envy. Somehow he couldn't envision getting that kind of cooperation from the lab in Austin. Maybe he could work out some kind of lend-lease program in investigative teams between New Mexico and the Texas Panhandle.

Lindman hung up the phone and turned to Charles. "They'll be here in about an hour and a half."

Charles rubbed his hands together. "Good. In the meantime, I'm going to do a little reading. Where did you put those books on archeology, Polanski?"

The inspector blinked. "That bag on the floor, Sheriff Matthews, but I still don't understand what you're looking for. I've certainly heard enough about archeology to satisfy any curiosity I had on the subject."

Charles emptied the bag and passed out books to Lindman, Polanski, and Raul. "Here, everybody help. I want to know how a dig is supposed to be organized. Bob James kept saying that there should have been more people. Dr. Hagan, after he was told that projectile points were found, started raving about calling in a team, about more archeologists. This whole case is about archeology. That's what brought Armijo to Folsom in the first place. It even accounts for the Leader being here."

Lindman interrupted. "How do you figure that?"

"Don't you think it's odd that shortly after the Leader arrives, he shows Bob James where to dig, and immediately James finds a—what was it called—balance stone? He helps at the dig until Armijo is murdered, then suddenly decides Folsom Man should keep his secrets. Why?"

"The murderer defiled the site, I guess," said Lindman, tapping his turquoise ring impatiently on the cover of a thick textbook. "For God's sake, Matthews, what are you saying?"

"The Leader is part of the conspiracy," Charles answered slowly.

Polanski sneezed violently and blew his nose. He looked at Charles with red, swollen eyes. "I don't see how you can infer that from the material I brought you."

"You're reaching, Matthews," said Lindman flatly.

"If I'm reaching, if everything is a coincidence, why did you bring me back to New Mexico?"

Lindman sat tapping his ring, his blue eyes frustrated. "Because a couple of hours after you show up in New Mexico someone hits you on the head. So I brought you back to see what else you can stir up, because somebody is scared of you. You're my bird dog, Matthews, and I want to see what you flush out."

Charles slapped him on the back. "Start reading, Sheriff. If we're going to break a conspiracy, we've got to know the jargon and then hit the weakest link in the chain of command."

"And who's that?" asked Lindman.

Charles looked at him. "David Lessing."

"He's the murderer?" asked Polanski.

"Either that, or the next victim. *Because he knows Raul isn't guilty.* Otherwise he wouldn't have been so careful to tell me that everybody had a motive."

"A guilty conscience," suggested Lindman.

"Or scared to death," said Charles.

17

THE BAR WAS solid oak, highly polished, elaborately carved, and eighteen feet long. Traditionally there should have been a painting of a plump nude hanging behind it. There wasn't. Instead Bob James had hung more framed artifacts. All that seemed to be missing from the hotel owner's collection was a mummy or two.

Charles sat down on one of the bar stools and rubbed a hand over his face. He'd entered the Folsom Hotel's bar to escape the commotion created by the arrival of the lab team and the State Police. He needed to clear his mind and to let the various pieces of information he'd accumulated arrange and rearrange themselves into patterns until, finally, a completed picture formed. He'd persuaded Lindman and Polanski that there was a conspiracy, and he'd better direct his questions to proving it. The conspiracy was the background of the picture and must be filled in if the central figures were to be understood. Then, and only then, could he isolate the murderer and have any chance of making his motive understood.

He rubbed his hands together, noticing that his palms were damp. Nervous tension, he decided. His theories were based on damn few facts, a hell of a lot of inference and a bit of amateur psychology. Even if everybody reacted as he hoped, he still couldn't prove a damn thing in court. The murderer would walk free unless the lab team could find some physical evidence to tie him to that atl-atl.

He wished Lindman would get back with the Leader and his band of followers. He could hear the lab team working diligently in the hotel parlor and envied their being busy. The hotel's occupants were also in the parlor, and he could hear the starts and fits of conversation that began and ended on the same sentence. It's hard to talk normally when two tall, black uniformed state police are listening to every word.

Charles glanced around the room and found himself trying to identify all the artifacts he saw with, what he suspected was, mediocre success. Two hours of cramming wasn't enough to pass a test. He finally focused on the projectile points hanging behind the bar. They looked familiar, and he sorted through the names he'd read: Yuma, Sandi, Clovis. He was concentrating so intently, he didn't hear the quiet movement behind him.

"Those are all Folsom points, Sheriff Matthews," said Bob James, going behind the bar and lifting a picture frame from the wall. Resting against a lining of red velvet were two rows of flint projectile points, each one bearing a groove down the center.

"You found all these?" asked Charles, wondering how the man had ever found the time to do anything with his life except dig.

Bob James had opened the frame, which Charles now noticed was hinged, and lifted out the longest point. "No. I traded for most of them and bought others. We collectors have shows every year where we buy and sell or trade artifacts. I've sunk all my money into this collection."

"It's quite a hobby then," said Charles, not sure he approved of such a market in what were, after all, antiquities.

"Hobby! A hobby is collecting bottle caps or beer cans. This is a religion; these are sacred objects we're protecting."

Bob James had a fanatical expression in his eyes, and Charles didn't like fanatics. In his opinion they ranked very close to serial murderers in their unpredictability. "Shouldn't they be in museums?"

"No!" The word was practically spat out, and Bob James bent over the artifacts like a monk protecting religious objects from rampaging heathens. He seemed to catch himself at the sight of Charles's expression and straightened. "Sorry, I didn't mean to yell at you, but you don't understand. Museums are like churches used to be back in the days when the Bible was chained to the pulpit and only the priest was allowed to read it. The priests are now the curators and archeologists, and only they are allowed to study and handle the artifacts."

"The church did that for the same reason museums keep valuable artifacts in locked cases: rarity and the chance that something irreplaceable might be lost," said Charles tartly.

Bob James had a pitying look on his face. "You just don't understand."

"I guess I don't," agreed Charles, glad to close the subject. However, he was premature in believing Bob James was ready to discuss anything but archeology.

"You see this flute or groove down the center of this projectile point?" he asked as his finger stroked it with a sensual delicacy that repulsed Charles. "There are three different theories about it. One is that the groove allows the blood to flow freely, causing the death of the animal more quickly. Also it leaves a bloody trail for the hunter to follow."

Charles swallowed. The thought of an animal running with one of those wicked little points buried in it until it bled to death made him nauseous. "What are the other theories?"

"One is that the spear shaft is split and the point is shoved in along the groove, then bound with sinew. The

140

last theory is that the longitudinal flake removed most of the weight of the point so the hunter got greater speed and distance. I like that theory myself because it fits in with my belief that Folsom Man had the atl-atl. See, a spear point was long and heavy because a man couldn't really throw it very far; it had to have some penetrating power. But these points, they're light and small, just the right size for a projectile dart. And sharp, my God, you wouldn't believe how these points will penetrate."

Charles swallowed again. "So it was one of these points that killed Armijo?"

Bob James closed the glass and replaced the picture frame on the wall. "One like it, I guess. I don't know; I haven't seen it."

"Can't you leave those things alone for one night?" Mary James's voice grated along Charles's nerve endings as if she'd actually touched him.

The hotel owner looked up at his wife as if mildly surprised at her reaction. "I was showing Sheriff Matthews what a Folsom Man point looked like. Not much else to do while we're standing around here waiting. Where'd Sheriff Lindman go, anyway?"

"To pick up the Skin People. We'd like everybody in one place, and since the hotel is larger than the Sheriff's office . . . "

Bob James chuckled. "Don't want to be in too close quarters with those folks. Wouldn't bother the FBI man though; I reckon he couldn't smell smoke if he was standing over a campfire."

"How can you laugh at a time like this? demanded his wife. "Policemen all over the hotel, that poor girl murdered. Doesn't it bother you at all?" Her blond braids had been combed out for the night, and her hair hung to her waist. She looked old and haggard.

"Sure it bothers me. Do you think I'm inhuman? But I can't undo anything. And neither can you," he added emphatically. "Why don't you make some coffee? I could use some, and I think maybe everyone else could too." His eyes focused on one of the lab man who'd just entered, and he rounded the bar at a trot. "Hey, watch out what you're doing! Those are stone axes in that case and they're over five thousand years old."

Wetting her lips, Mary James looked up at Charles. She opened her mouth as if to say something, but stopped abruptly and walked out. Charles turned, to see Raul coming through the doorway.

"I guess she still can't stand to look at me," said Raul. His soft voice was regaining some of its lilt.

Charles pushed a bar stool toward Raul. "Sit down. You look like you need a drink." Circling the bar, he poured two drinks—bourbon for Raul, brandy for himself. Silently he raised his glass in a toast. "Here's to catching your devil."

Raul took a sip of his drink. "Do you know who it is?"

"It's not you, so relax and enjoy Bob James's whiskey."

Raul smiled but Charles saw a flicker of hurt in his eyes. "I think sometimes you were not so sure."

His accent was stronger, an indication he was upset, and Charles debated the benefits of a merciful lie. He decided against it. He wasn't any better at lying to friends than he was at lying to himself. "I didn't doubt you as much as I doubted myself. I had to put my own house in order before I could help you. Once I did that, it was easy to believe in you."

Raul studied Charles, noticing that despite the deep grooves of fatigue on either side of his mouth, his eyes looked alert as if his mind were relieved of some intolerable burden. "Did you talk to Mrs. Lassiter when you were home today?"

Charles took a large swallow of his drink. He won-

142

dered if all his deputies were so damn good at reading him as Meenie and Raul were. "Yes," he replied.

Raul smiled like a man who fitted the last piece of a puzzle together. "That is what is different about you. I no longer feel L.D.'s spirit."

Charles set his glass down and limped around the bar to sit down. His thigh was aching badly. "Have you always been superstitious, or is it all this talk about Folsom Man and that damn volcano looming over the landscape? You sound like the Leader with his nonsense about spirits. Next thing I know, you'll be running around in buckskin pants and bare feet."

The front doors slammed open, and Lindman's outraged voice reverberated through the hotel. "Just march in here like good little boys and girls and don't give me any trouble. You too, Leader; your little game is over. Back to the purity of primitive man, huh? Throw off the corrupting influence of civilization? There were some parts of modern life you enjoyed, didn't you? The very worst parts."

Charles was off the bar stool and through the saloon doors into the parlor before Lindman had finished his tirade.

"I don't allow this poison"—he shook a small baggie in the Leader's face—"in my county. You damn hypocrite, I'll make you wish you'd never set foot in Union County."

The Leader stood with folded arms. "I know nothing about these drugs," he said, nodding at the baggie. "We have no need for chemical aids. Our knowledge can transport us to another level of existence."

"I'll transport you all right, you stinking bastard, and you can try another level of existence *in prison*."

He whirled around, his chin stuck out pugnaciously. "Any of you little disciples want to tell me about this, or would you rather be the Leader's cellmates?"

The band of followers seemed dazed. All but the redheaded one. "None of us take drugs. We even had to sign a pledge before the"—he hesitated—"Leader allowed us to join. He'd kick us out so fast we wouldn't have time to pack our atl-atls if we so much as smoked a little pot. I don't know where that stuff came from, but the Leader had nothing to do with it and neither did we. Somebody planted that stuff in the cave."

"And I suppose you have a candidate in mind?" asked Lindman sarcastically.

The boy nodded. "Armijo. He hated the Leader, and he knew just how to hurt him the most."

"Now what's that supposed to mean, young man?" demanded Lindman, his face still red.

Charles interrupted, his eyes fastened on the Leader as he spoke. "He means Faith was a drug addict; I saw the old needle tracks on her arms. Providing her with drugs would be an excellent way to punish you."

The Leader slumped onto a couch. "Yes," he admitted.

"I think we better move this interrogation upstairs," said Lindman firmly. "No sense in everybody hearing the story so they'll know how to back him up. Polanski, if you can drag yourself away from the lab team, we'd like you to accompany us. 'Tonio, can you see well enough to take notes?"

The young deputy snapped to attention, and peered at Lindman out of his one eye. He pushed his glasses back up his nose. "Yes, sir, as long as I look straight ahead." A state trooper snickered until Lindman turned and glared at him.

The Leader walked toward the stairs, a tall, commanding figure whose bizarre appearance didn't lessen his aura of authority. For an inexplicable reason, it was not he who was out of place, but everyone else. A state trooper hurriedly stepped back when the Leader brushed by him. Charles didn't blame him. Smelly antelope skin and all, it would take a brave man to challenge the Leader.

Sheriff Christopher "Kit" Lindman was a brave man. The door of Charles's room had barely closed when the lawman issued his challenge. "So Faith was an addict. Was Armijo slipping her drugs during their little sessions in his bedroom? Is that why you killed him?"

The Leader's shoulders slumped, and he looked old and shrunken. "Don't you think she would have screamed it to the skies if I had been the murderer? She hated me as much as she hated herself."

Lindman looked taken aback. "Why?"

The Leader sat down on the old wooden chair with the first awkward movement Charles had seen him make. "I committed her to a psychiatric ward for drug treatment. It saved her life, got her off drugs, but it wasn't her idea. It's like drying out an alcoholic; they have to want to be cured or it doesn't work. I brought her out here where I could control her environment, where even eating is a laborious process in which we must first catch our food. There are some scientific studies that show that emotionally disturbed people improve in a primitive environment where survival is a struggle."

"And the cave, the skin clothing, is a treatment program? Are all your followers emotionally disturbed?" asked Charles.

The Leader rested his elbows on his knees and covered his face with his hands. "No, they're perfectly normal."

"They just like living in a cave!" Lindman's voice was incredulous.

There was a pause. "It's a good learning experience," he said in a tone of irony.

"But the treatment wasn't working, was it?" asked Charles.

The Leader raised his head to look at him. "Armijo came. Dependent personalities gravitate to self-centered egotists like him, and they in turn feed on the weak. Finally I confronted him at the dig and warned him to leave her alone."

"When?" asked Charles.

"The day he was killed," replied the Leader, his expression telling Charles to make of his answer what he would.

"Warned him how? With a spear through his back?" asked Lindman.

The Leader's head swung to look at the sheriff. "I slapped him to the ground. I did not murder Armijo."

"What did Faith see when she left the circle?" asked Charles urgently.

The Leader's face twisted, whether with pain or bitterness, Charles couldn't decide. "I would be the last person she would tell. She blamed me for her misery. I forced her to face her life without the euphoria of her drugs, and she didn't like what she found."

"What was she to you?" asked Charles gently.

For the first time the Leader's eyes were vulnerable. "My daughter."

"Why did you bring her here?"

"To help cure her drug addiction."

Charles lashed out at the evasion. "But why here? Why Folsom, New Mexico? Why the little act with the skins and rituals in the crater of Mount Capulin? Why the band of followers? Why the interest in the dig?"

The older man's chin tipped up, his shoulders straightened. the grieving father figure was gone; the Leader was back. "Why not here? It's isolated, primitive."

Charles's voice softened, and anyone who knew him well would have recognized that he was most dangerous when he was the most quiet. "Have you ever heard of Linda Oberman?"

The average observer would have noticed no reaction to the question. Lindman, Charles, and even Polanski were not average observers. They saw the involuntary tremor of the Leader's fingers, saw the tiny pulse in his throat suddenly start to beat faster, saw the rapid tensing of his features in an effort to betray no emotion.

"No," he answered in a perfectly expressionless voice.

18

"HE'S LYING IN his teeth," said Lindman, clenching his own as he slammed the door behind the Leader. "I wish I'd had him hooked up to a lie detector when you asked him that last question. The needle would've jumped right off the graph."

Polanski sneezed. Other people cleared their throats when they were preparing to talk; Polanski sneezed. "What is it, Inspector?" Charles asked wearily.

"I really don't understand your interrogation procedures. Why did you let him go? In my opinion you should have continued; you had him on the defensive. At the bureau—"

"We haven't finished with the Leader," interrupted Charles hastily. He wasn't up to hearing what the bureau did. "But we weren't getting anywhere going up the middle, so we'll try an end-around play."

"I beg your pardon," said Polanski.

"Football, Polanski," said Lindman. "Don't you ever watch football?"

Charles took pity on the FBI agent. "The Leader won't tell us anything, and we don't have any evidence to confront him with, so we're going to question Dr. Hagan and David Lessing. They knew Linda Oberman, and it's reasonable to assume they'll know the Leader's connection to her."

"What does all this have to do with who killed Armijo and Faith?" asked Polanski stubbornly.

Charles sat down on the bed and rubbed his thigh. He

was desperately tired, too tired to give a lengthy explanation.

"Because three people lied about Linda Oberman, and I don't like lies of any kind in a murder investigation. And I don't believe in coincidence either," he said, eyeing Lindman. "Let's get them both up here together. Maybe they'll trip over one another's lies."

When 'Tonio escorted the two in, Charles stood up. "Gentlemen, we seem to be a little short of chairs, so if you'll sit on the bed, we're going to talk—about *Linda Oberman!*" His voice cracked like thunder in the quiet room.

David Lessing moaned and covered his face. Dr. Hagan sat down, staring sightlessly ahead.

"I've read the police report on Linda Oberman's suicide, Dr. Hagan. I've read your statement, and David's statement, and Armijo's statement. Now I want the whole story about the Colorado dig, and about Armijo's part in it. But most of all, I want to know what you and Lessing and the Leader were doing there. And no more lies."

Dr. Hagan's voice sounded hollow. "Linda Oberman was one of the most brilliant students of archeology I've ever had the privilege of teaching. If she'd lived, she might have accomplished more than her father. When I received the phone call from the curator of the Denver Museum of Natural History about the discovery of a large deposit of extinct bison bones mixed with Folsom Man projectile points, I naturally sent Linda to the site. I'll never forget how excited she was. Those big gray eyes of hers lit up. Did I tell you she was a beautiful girl? Beauty and brains."

There was a muffled sound from David Lessing, and Dr. Hagan sighed. "Linda couldn't direct the dig. That required a degree and experience, and she didn't have one, and not enough of the other, so I selected Enrique

Armijo. Sending him to Colorado with her was like asking a thief to guard the family jewels."

All of a sudden Charles felt old and tired. There wasn't anything complex about the motive after all. Enrique Armijo had slept with two different women, and both were women David Lessing loved. It even gave him a motive for murdering Faith, other than for his own survival. Betrayal was almost as old a motive for murder as sex and money.

He needed to finish the questioning, hear the rest of the answers, and he didn't want to. He heard Lindman take over and felt relieved.

With each question, Lindman slapped the top of one hand against the palm of the other. "What did happen in Colorado, Dr. Hagan? Why did Linda Oberman commit suicide? And I sure hope you're not going to tell me it was over Armijo, 'cause he wasn't worth the powder it'd take to blow him to hell, much less a young girl's life."

David jumped off the bed and stood with clenched fists, his eyes as tortured as an old man's that had seen many horrors. "No! At least not like you mean. And she didn't—"

"Sit down, David!" Dr. Hagan's voice was not to be disobeyed.

"I'm not going to let them think that Linda—"

Dr. Hagan grabbed David's wrist and jerked him down. "No more, David." He turned to Charles and spoke quickly, as though he was afraid he would be interrupted. "Linda was no match for Armijo. He simply led her around like a lamb. I visited the dig, and it was Enrique this and Enrique that. I wanted to turn her over my knee and apply the flat of my hand where it would do the most good. But I didn't. That was my first mistake. My second was not confronting Armijo, but I was afraid to wave a red flag in front of a bull. He was a master at retaliation, and I didn't want Linda hurt. I thought the fact that she was a special pupil of mine would protect her. As it turned out it didn't matter. He hurt her anyway."

"Then he jilted her and she committed suicide?" asked Lindman, continuing his rhythmic beat of hand against hand.

Dr. Hagan shifted and the rope bed creaked. "In a manner of speaking."

"Sure changed your tune some, didn't you, Dr. Hagan?" said Lindman. "According to the police report, you were frothing at the mouth, like a mad dog, about how she was murdered. Now all of a sudden it's seduction that got out of hand. I don't have any fancy letters after my name, but I've been sheriff in Union County for almost thirty years, and I don't have to touch cow manure to know that's what somebody's handing me. Now let's saddle up and ride down that road again."

"I was mistaken," replied Hagan, folding his arms and staring straight ahead again. "She was distraught because her dissertation was turned down."

David Lessing was on his feet in a single convulsive leap, the words erupting out of him. "Why are you lying?"

Dr. Hagan heaved himself off the bed and grasped David's shoulders. "Calm down, David; we were both wrong. Do you understand? We were both wrong," he repeated emphatically. "Don't say anything else."

The young man twisted away. "You're the one who doesn't understand, Dr. Hagan. It's too late; it's all over."

Hagan sank back on the bed, his eyes resigned, as though he had surrendered after losing a struggle he thought he could win.

David Lessing spoke directly to Charles, his words pouring out in a torrent of agony. "He stole her work, her dissertation on the Folsom Man culture and what happened to it. She told him about it during the Colorado dig and, God, Armijo couldn't stand it. His position as the authority on Folsom Man was being threatened by a *graduate student,* and a *woman* graduate student at that. He took her paper, rewrote it, and published it under his own name. The doctoral committee rejected her dissertation as being a copy of Armijo's article. She accused him of being a thief and a liar, and he killed her. You didn't know Armijo. No one crossed him."

Polanski sneezed again. "The Albuquerque police found no evidence of murder. The gun was lying by the body, the paraffin test on her fingers was positive, there were powder burns on her head—"

"She'd never shoot herself!" David burst out. "She hated guns! She was scared to death of them. It was almost a phobia with her; she'd freeze at the sight of anybody even holding one. She'd never shoot herself," he repeated. "Never."

He turned and pressed his forehead against the wall and took sobbing breaths as though he were a long distance runner whose race was over.

"Didn't you tell the police that?" asked Charles.

He turned around to face Charles. "Yes, but they wouldn't listen to us. I was a jealous boyfriend, and Dr. Hagan didn't want to believe his godchild would commit suicide. And Armijo was so damn smooth with his story about the dissertation, he made me sick."

He leaned against the wall again and pounded his fist against its plaster surface. "He killed her and nothing happened to him! But the police hauled me in to warn me about making 'slanderous remarks concerning Dr. Armijo.' It wasn't right, Sheriff Matthews; none of it was right."

Charles felt weary, so incredibly weary. "So to make things right you conspired to commit murder."

152

"No! That was not our intention. We were planning to ruin him."

"The dig," said Charles slowly as certain pieces of information arranged themselves into a pattern in his mind.

Dr. Hagan nodded. "Yes. We knew we could depend on Armijo's claiming credit for any finds made at the dig and publishing several articles about them. So we arranged for him to find something. One of his minor faults was lack of humility."

"You salted the dig," stated Charles flatly. "That's why there wasn't a complete archeological team on the site. You didn't dare try to fool too many people."

"You're very astute, Sheriff Matthews, but I think perhaps your term 'salted the dig' is more appropriately used in reference to a gold mine. We arranged for Armijo to find several intrusive artifacts, but without his realizing they were intrusive."

The professor sighed at the puzzled looks on the faces around him. "On an archeological dig, one of our most difficult tasks is dating an artifact. A piece of flint is a piece of flint, and its formation predates man. What concerns us is, At what time in the past did a man pick up that flint and chip flakes from it to form a projectile point? We must study each artifact *in situ*. If we find a projectile point stuck in the skull of a dead mammoth, we can fairly quickly assign a date to that point, because we know approximately when the mammoth became extinct. Also, radiocarbon testing of bones has proven very reliable. But that kind of find is rare and in my opinion impossible to fake well enough to fool an archeologist. And Armijo was a good archeologist."

Polanski interrupted. "If Armijo was such a skilled archeologist, why did he need to steal someone else's work?"

"He didn't steal her work, he stole her conclusions.

Linda was correlating every dig involving the Folsom Man culture and, using a computer, predicting the geographical range and sociological development of that culture. The Colorado dig was a campsite as well as a kill site, and in addition to projectile points, scrapers, and charred food bones, it also yielded carved stone beads, fetishes, and some evidence of a more highly organized social structure than found before. Her conclusions were exciting, controversial and, in my opinion, valid."

"So Armijo stole these conclusions, which makes him a common thief. How were you planning on catching him?" asked Lindman.

Dr. Hagan made a steeple of his fingers and slipped into his lecturing tone. "It was a challenging task. There are certain control standards that archeologists insist upon before considering any site to be deemed authentic. The data must come from a buried or sealed site, the artifact be found in a geological stratum of proven date—"

"What the hell does that mean?" demanded Lindman.

Dr. Hagan sighed again. Sheriff Lindman definitely had no aptitude for archeology. "If we find a projectile point in a gravel bed deposited during the last ice age, we can reasonably assume that projectile point is the same age as the gravel bed. It also helps if the artifact is found in association with extinct mammal remains, because we can get radiocarbon dates on bones. A really valuable site also contains distinctly recognizable artifact types. Folsom points are one such type. In order to discredit Armijo we had to make sure that in his mind, this site met all the requirements. So we simply let an amateur make the initial discovery."

"Bob James," said Charles.

"Yes. Bob had been corresponding about some wild theory or other with the university ever since he came

154

to New Mexico." The professor hesitated a second as if arranging his thoughts. "David came up to supervise the first stages of excavation until we reached the proper geological stratum, or level. Then we buried a bison bone, some points, and a few flakes to show that the hunters had taken the opportunity to make new points or sharpen old ones. We left them in the ground for a month." He rubbed his chin and glanced at Charles. "To age, you might say, and to let signs that the stratum had been disturbed disappear. David kept Bob James busy trenching in another area, and I kept Armijo on the leash by delaying sending him to the dig. The plan worked beautifully; Armijo never suspected the artifacts were actually intrusions in the stratum, that they had not originally been there."

"Quite a sacrificial lamb, aren't you, Dr. Hagan? You were going to discredit yourself when you announced that Armijo didn't know the real thing from a fake because you were going to have to explain how *you* knew it. Or did you have a plan to cover that problem?" Charles asked. He was glad Dr. Hagan hadn't taken to crime at an early age; the man was too clever.

"The artifacts he recovered belonged to Linda Oberman's father and were in her apartment the day she died. The bison bone has some identifiable cut marks on it, has already been photographed and listed on a cultural inventory list of another dig. The points were part of still another dig. When Armijo published his paper, Linda's father would step forward, and Armijo's career would be finished."

Lindman swore. "Your story's got more holes in it than a screen door." He blew out a deep breath and stood nose to nose with the professor. "So you were going to shake your finger and say 'naughty, naughty,' when Armijo started showing the artifacts around. Did you think he was so stupid he wouldn't suspect something when all the witnesses against him were involved with Linda Oberman?"

"That was a risk—" began Dr. Hagan.

"Risk! My aunt Stella's fanny! It was a sure thing. You and Lessing and Linda Oberman's father would have ended up being sued or arrested. But there was no risk if Armijo was dead, was there? You lured him up here to kill him. And what the hell kind of man is her daddy that he's letting you two do all the dirty work instead of whipping up on Armijo himself?"

"A very clever one," answered Charles quietly. "He's the Leader. Did he choose that title, Dr. Hagan, or did you?"

The professor sat back on the bed, an expression of hopelessness on his blunt features, while David tried to muffle a sob.

"I'll be damned," said Lindman softly. "Obvious as the nose on your face when you think about it."

'Tonio opened his mouth, a stunned expression on his face, but Polanski frowned him into silence.

"He was the leader of this conspiracy, wasn't he?" continued Charles. "He was the one who'd lost the most. He 'suggested' to Bob James where to dig, he salted the dig with his own artifacts, artifacts already reported as coming from another dig? He's an archeologist too, isn't he? That's why he knows so much about Folsom Man. And those kids must be students of his, probably enrolled in a field study course to learn more about Paleo-Indians by actually living as they did. The stage was set. You had the motive, the victim, innocent witnesses in the young students who could swear no one left the circle, and a scapegoat: Raul."

Charles's low, matter-of-fact voice cracked on his deputy's name, and he realized he had to finish up quickly before he lost control entirely. "The play came off beautifully. But then things began to go wrong. Faith left the circle and witnessed the murder, I came to New Mexico and started asking questions, and the most ironic thing of all, the dig turns out to be authentic."

Polanski let loose a gigantic sneeze. "Wait," he said, groping for a handkerchief and blowing his nose. "I believe Dr. Hagan testified that the dig was, er, salted."

"It was, Inspector," said Dr. Hagan earnestly. "But only with the bison bone, a few points, and the balance stone. The scraper, the seven projectile points, and the skeleton are real. My God, a skeleton. It's the most important discovery since the original Folsom dig. You just have no idea what it means." He clasped his hands together as if in prayer.

"I think I have a very good idea, Dr. Hagan. It provided a double motive for Faith's murder," said Charles. Only faint sounds from downstairs disturbed the absolute silence in the room as five pairs of eyes stared at him.

"What the hell are you talking about now, Matthews?" Lindman sounded impatient, if not downright testy.

"If her testimony had freed Raul, then the whole conspiracy would have been exposed, and who would believe that any of the artifacts at the dig were authentic? Not only was someone's survival at stake, but his reputation as well."

He straightened to his full six feet three and seemed even taller in the confines of the small room. "Now who killed Enrique Armijo and Faith?"

19

"EXCUSE ME, SHERIFF Lindman, but we're through downstairs. You ready for us to start up here?" An earnest looking young man wearing thick glasses stood in the open door.

Lindman's profanity was a mixture of Spanish and English with Norwegian still predominant. The young man swallowed, and his Adam's apple bobbed up and down like a rubber ball. "You did s—say you wanted to be kept informed of our progress," he stuttered.

Lindman pulled a handkerchief out of his pocket and wiped his face. "I did say that, didn't I? Well, get the team up here and get to work. Don't stand around holding up the doorway."

The lab man left, and Lindman stuffed his handkerchief back in his pocket. "Okay, Hagan, what have you got to say for yourself?"

Dr. Hagan stood up. He had used the interruption to recover his dignity and self-assurance, and it was with both that he spoke to Charles. "Regardless of what you and Sheriff Lindman think, we didn't plan to kill Armijo. We were as shocked as anyone at his murder. If you choose not to believe me, then think about this. Would any of us kill a man to avenge one sister, then turn around and murder the other sister? Would the Leader murder his own daughter? Would David, who's already lost one woman, kill another whom he also loved? Would I, at my age, be so desperate to save myself that I would murder a girl I held as a baby? I'm sorry, Sheriff

Matthews, but I think Raul killed Armijo because he's the only one with a motive and who didn't also love Faith."

He took David's hand and started leading him to the door as if he were a child. He turned back to look at Charles. "Rethink your premise, Sheriff; that's what every archeologist does when the artifacts don't fit the theory. We'll be downstairs if you need us, but I think we'd be most unwise to talk to you again without an attorney present."

Lindman stood looking at the closed door. "Damn it to hell, but he's right, Matthews. I can't see the Leader stabbing his own daughter, not even to escape a murder charge, and I never have believed Hagan did it. Lessing, I just don't know."

Charles sat down on the bed. "Inspector, what did you find in Armijo's Albuquerque home?"

Polanski pulled a small spiral notebook from his pocket. " 'Arrived with officer from Albuquerque Police Department at residence of Enrique Armijo at 11:05 ...' "

"I don't care what time you got there or if you took the Wicked Witch of the West with you, I want to know what you found," snapped Charles.

Polanski sneezed. "Nothing."

"The dog that didn't bark."

"I don't believe Armijo had a dog. We found no evidence to that effect."

Charles closed his eyes and prayed for patience. "That was a line from Sherlock Holmes," he explained. "What I mean is that you found no journals."

"We don't know that there were any more journals," began Polanski.

"There must have been. He was a man who recorded every thought he had. If he filled four notebooks while on this dig, then it was a habit. Don't you think it odd that you didn't find any at his home?"

"Maybe he kept them in a safety deposit box," suggested 'Tonio, who quickly stuck his nose back in his own notebook as he found himself on the receiving end of three frowns.

"So what happened to them?" asked Lindman.

"Dr. Hagan's little trip to Albuquerque, the one he made after the murder. The conspiracy had to cover its tracks. I'm guessing that they were afraid Armijo had kept a complete record of the Colorado dig and the subsequent charges and counter charges that resulted. They couldn't risk someone reading those journals and asking questions. The investigation into Linda Oberman's death was closed, and they didn't want to give the police any reason to reopen it."

"Which means," said Lindman with the beginning of enthusiasm in his voice, "that either Dr. Hagan committed the murder or someone told him. Otherwise, how did he know to leave for Albuquerque?"

"Exactly," said Charles. "And we know that Raul wouldn't stop by the professor's room and casually announce he'd just knocked off Armijo, and neither would Bob James."

"And that leaves David Lessing."

"Just a minute," interrupted Polanski. "If your theory is correct, why didn't they take Armijo's journals out of his room here at the hotel?"

Lindman and Charles looked at each other. It was a good question; in fact, it was a chasm right through the middle of their case.

"Their only opportunity was the night of the murder, and I guess Dr. Hagan was too anxious to get to Albuquerque to do it himself," said Lindman slowly.

"And if David Lessing had just murdered a man, I doubt he was in any condition to do it," added Charles.

"And by the time Dr. Hagan got back Saturday night, I had a man stationed here until I could get back with the search warrant. Took the whole damn night, too. I had to track down the judge to sign it. By Sunday, Raul had been arrested. Why arouse suspicion by searching the room, when the suspected murderer was already in jail?"

"But someone did," objected Polanski.

"They had no choice, because I came," said Charles. "They had to get rid of those journals."

"So which one do we arrest?" asked 'Tonio eagerly.

Charles looked at 'Tonio's young face and felt older than the skeleton still half buried in the dirt of centuries. "Let's go talk to the Leader," he said and walked out the door.

'Tonio was so close behind him, Charles could feel his breath on the back of his neck. "It was him all the time, huh? That's terrible, Sheriff Matthews. I mean, what's worse than a man who'd kill his own daughter?"

"A man who'd manipulate someone else into doing it for him," Charles replied and walked down the stairs.

The scene in the parlor had changed little. Dr. Hagan and David Lessing shared the couch with Mary James, while Raul hovered unobstrusively behind it, unnoticed and unwanted. All were silent, locked into their own little spheres of personal space, not touching, not even looking at one another.

In contrast, Bob James was standing in front of a display case with the Leader's students clustered around him like dirty little puppies. "Mary's always after me to stop grubbing around for 'pieces of rock,' as she calls them, and to trace my ancestors, but I'm not anxious to do that. Who knows? I might be related to the Jesse James gang. I don't think I really want to know, so I just study Indian cultures instead. I know I'm not an Indian."

"I wish you were. Then none of this would've happened and that poor girl would still be alive." Mary

James cried suddenly. Scrambling to her feet, she ran sobbing toward the kitchen.

Bob James cleared his throat. "We never had any kids, and she kind of adopted Faith and young David here." Reaching out, he absently stroked the display case. "I'd better go see about her, I guess. She just doesn't understand." He wandered out of the room.

"His wife'd be better off if she were shaped like an arrowhead; at least he'd notice her more," commented Lindman. He jerked his head at Charles. "Let's finish this up."

Charles circled the couch and touched Raul's arm. "Hang in there, *amigo*."

Raul looked at the tall figures in the black uniforms of the New Mexico state police stationed around the room and smiled bitterly. "Do I have a choice?"

Suddenly there was a roar from Lindman, directed at the young trooper who had been guarding the Leader. "What the hell do you mean by letting him outside, you idiot?"

"I'm glad it wasn't me," muttered 'Tonio from the vicinity of Charles's left shoulder.

The trooper backed away from the irate sheriff until he bumped into the wall. "He can't get away; Johnson's out there with him. You don't know how it was, sir. He kept standing so close, and God, he smelled. Johnson said he'd take him outside so he could at least get upwind."

"Young man, you'd never make it in the FBI," said Polanski.

"Shut up, Polanski. Lindman, chew the kid out later," ordered Charles as he jerked open the hotel's double doors.

The state trooper, Johnson, straightened to attention and licked his lips at the sight of Lindman's face. "He's right here, sir. I've kept my eye on him the whole time."

162

Lindman jerked his thumb toward the hotel. "Why don't you get in there and keep your eye on his little band. And I don't care if you have to hold your breath while you do it."

"Damn kids," he muttered to Charles as the young trooper scurried inside. "Don't have any business in law enforcement if they can't stand a little odor. God knows, most of the people we arrest stink one way or another."

Charles ignored him as light flooded through the open doors and spotlighted the Leader. He squatted on the ground, holding his atl-atl upright at his side, Mount Capulin looming in the distance behind him. For a second his eyes seemed to glow red in the reflected light.

"Dr. Oberman, I presume," said Charles, striding across the porch with Lindman and Polanski behind him.

Using his atl-atl as a crutch, the Leader levered himself up. "It's just as well that you know who I am. I find my role is becoming too real."

"Which role?" Charles spat out the words. "That of leader of a bunch of kids playing Indian, or that of leader of a conspiracy?"

The Leader's head jerked around. "I am found out indeed." He tightened his hold on the atl-atl. "I never meant for it to turn out this way."

"Didn't you? Perhaps Dr. Hagan believes that, possibly even David, but Lindman and I don't. You set up the conspiracy, not to ruin Armijo, but to murder him."

"Yes," agreed the Leader. "But it wasn't to be murder; it was to be an execution."

"And was there a trial? Did Armijo have an attorney? Did you examine the evidence objectively? Dr. Hagan says your daughter had an affair with Armijo; David Lessing denies it. The two of them can't even seem to agree on whether your daughter Linda's death was suicide or murder."

"It was murder!" said the Leader, his eyes black and compelling.

"You don't know that, not beyond a reasonable doubt, and that's what you have to prove in a murder trial. So don't call yourself an executioner instead of a murderer."

"I'm not," replied the Leader quietly. "Because the conspiracy failed; none of us killed Armijo."

Charles grabbed one of the wooden posts that supported the porch roof and squeezed it between his hands. He wished it were the Leader's throat. "You're a liar, damn you! Faith saw one of the conspirators at Capulin. That's why she wouldn't talk. She didn't run away because I was questioning her; she ran when you appeared. If Raul were the murderer, why not say so in front of you? But if it were a member of the conspiracy, it wouldn't be safe, would it?"

The Leader bit his lip and began shaking his head slowly from side to side. "No! That's not true. She just didn't understand. David found her leaning over the body in an almost catatonic state. She saw him appearing out of the darkness like the worst kind of specter, and she was terrified. In Faith's mind, seeing David and finding Armijo's body were linked, cause and effect."

"Smart girl," remarked Lindman. "Why else would he be at the crater except to dispose of Armijo?"

The Leader looked toward Capulin again. "He followed her back to the circle and motioned to me to end the ritual," he said finally.

Lindman prefaced his response to that remark with a profanity that was short, obscene, and in English. "Wait a minute. Why didn't those kids see him?"

"They are in deep self-hypnosis during a ritual; they

wouldn't notice someone far outside the circle who was silent."

"So what happened next?" asked 'Tonio, glancing quickly toward Lindman to see if the sheriff would object to his asking a question.

"I was planning to make an excuse to stay behind for a few moments, but that was unnecessary. We stumbled over the body, and Faith became hysterical. I sent her back to the cave with the others, telling them I would notify the park rangers. When they were over the rim of the crater, I called to David. He was huddled against a lava boulder, trembling and nearly in shock."

"Being a murderer bothers some people," observed Lindman cynically.

"What did you do?" asked Charles.

The Leader closed his eyes, then opened them to reveal the first regret Charles had seen him reveal. "I slapped him. I had no time for hysterics. I asked him what happened, and he denied murdering Armijo. I believed him. I sent him back to the hotel to awaken Dr. Hagan."

"So Hagan could go to Albuquerque to search for Armijo's journals?" asked Charles.

The Leader inclined his head. "You are formidable, Sheriff Matthews. You seem to know all the answers already."

Charles felt no triumph, just a hatred so deep, it pressed on his mind like a heavy weight. "You sick, arrogant bastard. You manipulated everyone: Armijo, David, Dr. Hagan, Bob James, even your own daughter. Faith, as much as the salted artifacts, was the bait to keep Armijo at the dig."

A flickering of self-loathing appeared in the Leader's eyes, and Charles knew he'd guessed correctly. "But you miscalculated; you forgot you were dealing with real people. You couldn't keep your daughter away from

Armijo any more than you could keep a moth from the flame. So you warned him off, slapped him down in front of the whole dig. You also did one other thing: you exposed the affair to everyone. Seeing Faith fall in love with Armijo was the breaking point for David Lessing. He committed murder, and Faith saw him. *And you knew it.*"

The Leader took careful steps to the porch and sank down. "He was almost my son," he said softly, looking up at Charles. "Wouldn't you protect your son?"

"Not at the expense of someone else's son," replied Charles.

The Leader lowered his head until his chin rested on his chest. Finally he grasped the porch railing and pulled himself up as slowly as though he were an old, old man. "I want to see David's face."

'Tonio held open the double doors and the Leader started through, then hesitated and put his hands on either side of the door frame. His head sank onto his chest again, and Charles could see his shoulders heave with repeated deep breaths. Finally his tall figure straightened and he walked through with the lawmen following him.

Dr. Hagan blinked slowly at the expression on the Leader's face, then closed his eyes and leaned his head back against the couch. David Lessing reared up, his face stiff and old-looking beyond his years. "Leader?" he asked, but his eyes were already dull with resignation.

"Sheriff Lindman!" The same lab technician with the thick glasses and prominent Adam's apple clattered down the stairs.

Lindman ground his teeth together. "What is it?" he asked, his voice close to a snarl.

The lab man swallowed. "Uh, we found it. It was in the back of an old clothes press, I think it's called."

Lindman grabbed the man's arm. "You sure?"

The man looked insulted. "Reasonably sure. Of course, someone could have gutted a rabbit, or stood in that piece of furniture to shave and nicked their chin, but I don't think it's likely. It wasn't much and we had to scrape it up, and I'll still need to run some tests, type it, and so forth, but I'm pretty sure it's human blood."

Lindman pushed him toward the front doors. "Run to Clayton and use Doc Garcia's lab. And hurry up, damn it."

"What room did you find it in?" asked Charles urgently.

The lab man scratched his head. "Uh, it was the middle room on the south side. I guess it'd be Number 2."

Mary James screamed, a keening sound that seemed to rise and fall in monotonous waves. Her husband clapped his hand over her mouth and half dragged her to a chair by the stairwell.

The Leader lifted his arms and reached toward David, then let them fall to his sides. "Why didn't you trust me, David? I would've made Faith understand. You didn't have to kill her."

"You bastard!" Raul launched himself over the back of the couch and closed his hands around David Lessing's throat.

20

THERE WAS A split-second pause before Charles shook off the paralysis of mind and body caused by the suddenness of seeing peace-loving Raul actively trying to strangle a man. "Raul, stop!" he shouted and, shoving the Leader aside, dove for his deputy.

He was too late; Dr. Hagan reacted first. The chunky old professor wrapped his huge fingers around Raul's wrists and squeezed. Within seconds Raul grunted with pain and released David's throat. David slumped sideways on the couch, his own hands clawing at his throat in an effort to breathe.

"There has been enough violence," announced Dr. Hagan in a stern tone.

He looked around the room at the silent faces, examining each one, from the lab men standing with their mouths open, to the Leader's band with their somber expressions, to Charles, and finally, the Leader. He stared longest at the Leader, and Charles sensed a message sent and received, and control relinquished by the Leader and accepted by Dr. Hagan.

"Whatever the outcome of this discovery of human blood in David's room, Dr. Oberman"—he nodded toward the Leader—"and I bear full responsibility."

Charles broke in, his voice harsh. "Very noble, Dr. Hagan, and very true. But unfortunately it doesn't help David Lessing. You and Oberman will go back to your quiet world of archeology, maybe a little tarnished once the conspiracy is explained during the trial, but you'll survive. You won't be spending the rest of your life in prison, where someone tells you when to eat and when to sleep, and where every door you see is locked."

Charles could feel a pulse pounding in his temple and knew he was close to losing all control. He ground his teeth together at the utter waste of three lives because two old men chose to play vigilante. He switched his attention to Oberman. "David threw that atl-atl, but you all but put it in his hand. If he doesn't damn you, I will."

David Lessing pushed himself to a sitting position on the couch. Livid splotches on his neck marked where Raul's fingers had pressed into his flesh. "I didn't murder Armijo—"

"Hush, David," cautioned Dr. Hagan. "Don't say anything else until we get you a lawyer."

David looked at Dr. Hagan, and an expression of hurt and disillusionment crept across his face, like a noxious ground fog, killing innocence and hope. "You think I did it, don't you? Well, I didn't, and I'm not going to wait for a lawyer either." He rested his face in his hands for a moment. "I'm so tired of lying," he said, his voice muffled.

"David Lessing, I arrest you for the murder of Enrique Armijo and Faith Oberman." Sheriff Lindman pulled a card from his billfold. " 'You have the right to remain silent. Anything you say can and will be used against you in . . . ' "

David Lessing listened impatiently until Lindman had finished. "I understand what you're telling me but I still don't want a lawyer. I want to tell you about it."

"David! No!" cried the Leader.

David ignored him, looking at Charles instead. "You were right when you called this whole plot a murder conspiracy."

Lindman grabbed his arm. "Hold it, son. Are you making a confession?"

David shook his head. "No, because I didn't kill anybody, but I'm going to tell you what happened. It's up to you to figure out who did it."

"O.K.," Charles said. "Let's hear your story, David."

David's tense posture relaxed slightly, and he looked up at Charles. "You were right, Sheriff Matthews. This was a conspiracy to murder Armijo."

"David! That's not true!" protested Dr. Hagan.

David glanced over Charles's shoulder at the Leader. "We never told you, Dr. Hagan; we knew you'd never agree." He shifted on the couch to face the old professor. "Ruining Armijo wasn't enough, not for what he did."

Dr. Hagan's square body seemed to lose its shape as he slumped back on the couch. "Oh, God, David, he didn't kill Linda. It was an—an accident; it was in the journals I stole out of his house in Albuquerque. She called him over to her apartment and accused him of destroying her life, first with the affair, then with his theft of her work. She was waving the gun around threatening to kill him and then herself." He looked at Charles. "She was like her father, very dramatic. But she wasn't familiar with guns. She didn't know the safety was off. The gun went off and she died."

"Oh, my god!" The Leader staggered to the staircase and sank onto the steps. His crowd of students murmured among themselves while the State Policemen moved closer to the couch. Mary James still sat in the chair where her husband had dragged her. Tears ran down her cheeks in silent streams, and she rocked back and forth, her arms wrapped around herself. Bob James had moved to the front doors where he stood looking out at Capulin, a cigar clenched in his teeth.

David Lessing sat absolutely still, his eyes like two black, lifeless coals in a bloodless face. "It's not true," he whispered.

Dr. Hagan started to touch David's shoulder, but

hesitated and let his hand fall limply onto the back of the couch. "I'm sorry, David. I should have told you before, but Armijo was already dead, and it didn't seem to matter any more."

David finally moved and rubbed his palms on his denim-covered thighs. "It was still Armijo's fault."

Lindman's face looked as sick as Charles felt. "So you followed him to Capulin and killed him? Is that right, David?"

David licked his lips. "I followed him, but I didn't kill him."

"Don't tell me you were showing him your atl-atl and it just happened to go off," said Lindman sarcastically.

Charles frowned at Lindman. The stress was beginning to fray everyone's temper, and the Clayton sheriff was no exception.

"I didn't have an atl-atl," insisted David.

Lindman's face was beginning to turn red and Charles interrupted. "David, what happened after you decided to follow Armijo?"

David turned to Charles with the gratitude of a small child. "I went upstairs to my room to wait. I knew the ritual wouldn't start until around midnight; the Leader had to be sure the park rangers were all asleep. I turned off my light, lay on my bed, and listened for his footsteps. The hall is hardwood, and it creaks wherever you step" He stopped and rubbed his fingers across his forehead. "I lay there and thought about all the reasons for killing Armijo: what he'd done to Linda and what he was doing to Faith and what he was going to do to Raul. He was a—a wrecker; he destroyed lives with no more thought of what he was doing than one of those cranes swinging a steel ball into the side of a building. Someone had to stop him."

He rubbed his palms against his thighs again, and beads of sweat on his forehead glistened in the overhead light. "I imagined how it would feel to kill him, and wondered if there'd be much blood and if I could stand to touch him afterwards. And I would have had to touch him, because it had to look like an accident . . . "

"An accident? With a dart through his chest?" asked Lindman with skepticism.

"I wasn't going to kill him that way; I was going to hit him in the"—he swallowed—"head and then roll him down the side of the crater. It's steep and covered with lava boulders in most places. But I kept thinking about touching him, and I started to shake. It was warm in my room, but I was lying on my bed shaking with cold. And sick, I was so sick. I finally curled up under the covers and tried to blank out my mind, to think of nothing at all."

He started laughing, a high, toneless sound that made Charles grit his teeth. The laughter stopped as if someone had flipped a switch. "It's so funny," he said, looking at Charles. "I blanked out my mind so well I went to sleep."

He closed his eyes and rested his head against the back of the couch. "I think I wanted to sleep forever."

"Armijo woke you when he walked past your room?" asked Polanski.

David shook his head. "No, something woke me about midnight, a door closing, I think. I panicked when I realized I'd gone to sleep. I grabbed my coat and ran downstairs as quietly as I could and out the front door. I started toward Capulin. I felt like I was the only person alive in the world. It was dark and there were patches of ground fog, and Capulin, always Capulin, waiting just in front of me. I stopped and listened several times, but I couldn't hear Armijo ahead of me. I was scared by that time, and I was ready to believe he could see in the dark like a cat. How else could he avoid falling over rocks and rough spots the way I was doing? I finally gave up trying to be quiet and just ran. It took a long time to climb the side of the crater, and I kept kicking small pieces of lava, and they'd roll down the crater. I was loud, and I was breathing so hard, my chest hurt. I got to the top of the crater and stood on the path that winds around the rim and looked inside. It was a black yawning hole with only the Leader's fire at the very bottom. I started down into the crater. I couldn't see anything, not the shrubs, or the boulders, and I stumbled and fell several times."

He ran his fingers through his hair nervously. "About halfway down I saw Faith leave the circle. I could see her plainly, or at least her silhouette, because she was standing up and was between me and the fire. I started towards her, and that's when I found her crouched over the body. I scared the hell out of her, and she started crawling away from me. I called out that it was David and not to be afraid."

David looked at the floor, then back at Charles. There were tears glazing his eyes. "I was relieved," he burst out. "I didn't want to kill him, hadn't even brought a weapon with me. I don't think I'd have killed him even if I had. I was so glad somebody else had done it. Then I got scared again. We'd be blamed, we'd go to prison. I didn't want to go to prison for killing Armijo; I just wanted to forget the whole thing."

"So you told the Leader you didn't do it, and he sent you back to wake up Dr. Hagan so he could go to Albuquerque," said Lindman.

David nodded. "Yes, and then I went back to the hotel and was sick in the bathroom.

"I'd like to ask a question that's been puzzling me," Polanski said. "Why didn't you search Armijo's room here? If we hadn't found those journals, our suspicions would never have been aroused, and it's doubtful if we'd have ever discovered the conspiracy. Or at least, not so easily."

"But we did!" exclaimed David. "Dr. Hagan searched his room that night before he left for Albuquerque. There were no journals there."

Charles jerked at David's answer, his assumptions thrown into chaos.

Lindman slapped his hand on the marble-topped coffee table. His turquoise ring made a sharp cracking sound, and David Lessing flinched. "Then why did you search the room again two days later and knock Sheriff Matthews here in the head?"

"I didn't!"

Lindman put his hands on his hips and grimaced with disgust. "And you're a damn liar. You searched Matthews's room, found out he was a sheriff, and hightailed it into Armijo's room to get those journals."

David sat mute, his lips tightly closed, but his face was flushed.

The Clayton sheriff turned his back, his face as red as David's, and took a deep breath. He let it out slowly and turned back. "And now I suppose you're going to tell me there wasn't an atl-atl in your room."

"There was, but I didn't put it there. I found it Saturday morning. God, I didn't know what to do; there were sheriff's deputies all over the place. I couldn't leave the hotel with it. You rounded us all up and kept us downstairs to take our statements. I thought after I gave mine that I could go upstairs and move that atl-atl, throw it out the window or something. But then the call came from Sante Fe and you rushed off to search the crater for it. But you left a man here, and I still couldn't do anything. I had to sit downstairs and think about that gory thing leaning in the corner of the clothes press."

"Who did you tell?" asked Charles.

"Nobody! Dr. Hagan was gone, and I couldn't get

174

away to talk to the Leader until Sunday. I never did tell him about the atl-atl, though."

"Why?" asked Charles.

"I didn't know who to trust. I didn't know who had put that atl-atl in my room except it was someone who knew I'd been at Capulin. Dr. Hagan knew, and the Leader."

David wiped his wrist across his forehead, leaving a dry streak. He took a deep breath before he continued, his voice beginning to crack and waver. "Sheriff Lindman left for a search warrant, and I knew I was trapped. The deputy sent us upstairs to sit in our respective rooms; I guess he figured an atl-atl was too big to flush down the toilet. I went to my room, jerked open the door to that clothes press; I don't know what I had in mind exactly, setting fire to it maybe. But it was gone."

"It sure was. You walked across the hall and put the damned thing in Raul's closet," said Lindman.

"No, I didn't! I tell you it just disappeared!"

"Now listen, son, we ain't playing Hunt the Thimble," snapped Lindman. "Raul certainly didn't get that atl-atl out of your clothes press and put it in his. You're the only one who knew where it was, so you're the only one who could've done it, and I'm gonna have my deputy's hide for not watching you closer."

David got up and clutched Lindman's arm. "I don't know who put that atl-atl in my room, and I don't know who took it out. You've got to believe me."

"Yeah," said Lindman sourly, "like I believe in the tooth fairy."

"*I* moved it."

Charles jerked around. Mary James stood by her chair, looking old and desperate. "Why?" he asked. "And why did you put it in Raul's room?"

She walked over to David and stroked his head. "I went upstairs Saturday morning to put out fresh towels and straighten the rooms. I found the atl-atl while I was hanging up some of David's clothes. I wasn't going to let David go to jail."

"But you didn't care if Raul did, though. Why, damn it, why? Why hurt someone you didn't even know, who hadn't done anything to you? Didn't you even think how cruel your action was?"

She looked at Charles with an expression of desperation mixed with resignation. "What else could I do? I had to keep the sheriff away from David, and the best way to do it was to make sure they suspected someone else. Who else was there? Dr. Hagan? The Leader? My husband? Besides, I knew Raul was a deputy sheriff; I thought the law would take care of its own."

"Is that what you're doing now? Taking care of your own?" asked Charles.

Mary James's eyes closed for a moment, and Charles watched her wring her hands. "It's the truth." She opened her eyes. "I did what I had to do."

David Lessing covered his face with his hands. Raul, standing at Dr. Hagan's end of the couch, threw his head back and looked toward the ceiling as though asking God if his misery had ended.

"God in heaven, woman!" Lindman exploded. "You tampered with evidence."

"Did searching my room come under the heading of taking care of your own?" asked Charles. "And assaulting me?"

"What? That was Lessing!" said Lindman, his mouth falling open.

Charles watched Mary James as he spoke to Lindman. "We assumed it was Lessing because Mary James said she heard him come through the front door. We've made a good many assumptions about this case on the basis of her testimony, yet we've never questioned anything she said. She's an agile woman. She could have easily climbed down that tree and come into the house through the kitchen."

"No! I didn't hit you!" she cried, looking wildly around the room. "I'm not that kind of a person."

Charles nodded slowly. "You don't have the character, you mean. You did search my room, though, didn't you? It would have been in character for someone so desperately protecting her people. And you told David who I was. You also told someone else, didn't you? But that was a mistake, because he put the journals back in Armijo's room; we found them, and David Lessing was under suspicion again. There was nothing you could do this time, was there? You screamed that Raul was a criminal, you tried to throw me out of the hotel, but the only real way you could help David was to tell the truth." Charles looked at her with pity. "You have no choice; and whatever you decide, you won't ever enjoy living with the decision."

"I fail to understand what your point is, Sheriff Matthews," said Polanski. "We have physical evidence on Lessing; we have witnesses to Mrs. James's testimony. What kind of a choice are you giving her?"

Charles reached out and took her hand. Her skin was dry and scaly, her cuticles cracked, hard callouses marched across her palms. It was the hand of a woman who spent the majority of her day doing hard physical labor. Mary James, he knew, was maid, and cook, and hostess for the whole hotel.

He squeezed her hand. "You aren't any safer than Faith."

"No! He didn't kill Faith!" cried Mary James. She plucked at Charles's sleeve and shook her head slowly from side to side. "He didn't kill Faith."

"If he killed Armijo, then he killed Faith," said Charles. "The two go together."

Mary James stared at him, her eyes dull and frightened looking, and shook her head.

"Damn it to hell, Matthews, what are you talking about?" roared Lindman.

Charles turned. Capulin still occupied the greater part of the horizon visible through the open doors, and cold air still eddied through them and across the floor. But the balding hotel owner was gone.

21

CHARLES GRABBED A fistful of shirt belonging to the state policeman nearest to the door. "Bob James! Where did he go?"

"Bob James!" Lindman exclaimed. "Are you crazy, Matthews? What the hell was his motive?"

"Archeology," said Charles as he gave the trooper a shake. "Where is Bob James?"

The state policeman blushed a bright red. "I don't know. I moved up to listen to the lady, and I don't know where he went."

Charles pushed the trooper aside. "Raul, you and 'Tonio keep these people here." He started for the door. "Lindman, Polanski! Come on. We've got to find him."

Lindman seized Charles's shoulder. "We aren't going anywhere, at least not until I have some answers."

"Damn it, Lindman, not now! We don't have time." Charles looked past Lindman toward the staircase, and his face went blank. "Where's the Leader?"

Lindman whipped around. "Where's the Leader?" he yelled.

A state policeman with the height of a basketball guard and the neck of a football lineman made a valiant attempt to fade into the woodwork by the staircase. It was not successful. Lindman climbed three steps until he was level with the trooper's face and leaning over the bannister, grabbed his lapels, giving a vicious little twist that sawed the collar into the man's neck. Lindman stuck his face to within an inch of the trooper's. "Where is the Leader?"

Charles thought the trooper's eyes were beginning to protrude, but it was always possible he had a thyroid condition. The wheezing breaths he was taking and the bluish color around his mouth did indicate a more serious problem, however. "Lindman, ease up," said Charles, grabbing his arm. "You're strangling him."

The trooper gave Charles a grateful look and proceeded to undo his collar, lean against the wall, and take several deep breaths. "I'm sorry, sir," he panted. "About halfway through your questioning he got up. He didn't move though, just stood up. I didn't notice him after that. But he didn't come by me; I could swear to that."

"You big idiot! You were watching the show just like that damn fool by the door. A herd of buffalo could have walked by you, and you wouldn't have noticed anything until one of them butted you in the behind."

"He walked out the front door about five minutes ago," volunteered the redheaded student.

"Why the hell didn't you stop him?" Lindman's voice had degenerated to a snarl.

The young man gulped. "You don't tell Dr. Oberman what to do."

Charles could easily believe that. He turned and headed toward the door, his long legs covering the distance in a few steps. He vaulted off the porch in a dead run, fumbling in his pocket for the keys to Bob James's jeep. "Come on, Lindman!" he screamed.

Lindman roared out of the door followed by Polanski and the state police. "Wait a damn minute, Matthews!"

Charles climbed in the jeep, started the engine, and turned the vehicle in a tight circle, peering through the windshield as the headlights illuminated the harsh landscape. The moon was full and hung low in the sky above Capulin. He could hear motors revving up as the state troopers climbed into their patrol cars. He pounded the steering wheel in frustration. "Which way, damn it? Which way would he go?"

Lindman scrambled over the side into the front seat while Polanski dived ungracefully into the back. "Hell, I don't know," answered Lindman. "But I do know one thing. You'd better be right this time."

Polanski sneezed and tapped Charles on the shoulder. "I saw a shadow move."

"Where?" shouted Charles and Lindman in unison.

Polanski pointed. "Straight ahead toward Capulin."

Charles rammed the accelerator to the floor and the jeep lurched ahead, throwing Lindman into the dashboard and Polanski half over the front seat. There was a metallic scream as the jeep tore through a barbed wire fence. Lindman's voice was a high pitched squeal of protest. At least, Charles assumed it was a protest; not speaking Norwegian himself, he couldn't be sure.

"Damn it to hell, Matthews, you just drove through somebody's fence." He sat up and pushed at Polanski. "Get back there and hang on. This damn fool's gonna kill us both, and I don't even know why."

"It was all in the journals, but we looked for a motive we understood. Bob James counted on that, and he was right. Do you see anything, Polanski?" he asked abruptly.

The inspector grabbed the back of the seat and stood up. "Yes! Straight ahead! Can you see him?"

Huge lava squeeze-ups dotted the plain, elongated shadows bulging from the base of each to spread inky blotches across the ground. The Leader's eerie figure was silhouetted against the backdrop of Capulin. He twisted to glance over his shoulder, an action that saved his life. A flash of light no larger than a firefly winked in the darkness ahead and the sharp crack of a rifle seemed to echo off Capulin's crater. The Leader's body jerked backward, then crumpled.

"He shot him! And right in front of me!" Lindman sounded as if he couldn't believe the hotel owner could be so audacious.

Charles shifted to a lower gear and the jeep bounced forward over the uneven ground until the headlights revealed the Leader's body. "Damn fool!" he cursed as he slammed on the brakes.

Vaulting out of the jeep, he knelt, his fingers immediately pressing against the side of the Leader's throat, feeling for a pulse. "Come on, you arrogant bastard, be alive."

The Leader's voice was husky as if his throat was clogged. "Help me up."

"Where'd he hit you?"

"The shoulder," he replied. "If I might borrow a shirt to bind it, I'll be fine."

Charles stripped off his coat and unbuttoned his shirt. "We'll send you back with one of the state troopers."

"What the hell were you trying to do?" demanded Lindman, ripping Charles's shirt into strips.

"He killed Faith!" said the Leader, his eyes glittering like liquid in the jeep's headlights.

"There is also the matter of Armijo," said Polanski.

The Leader shrugged and caught his breath in pain. "Armijo deserved to die," he panted.

"I'm getting mighty tired of you trying to do my job for me," said Lindman, his eyes doing a little glittering of their own.

"I take care of my own."

"That's gotten two people killed already," said Charles grimly as he folded several strips from his shirt into a pad. The Leader held it over his wound while Charles tied it in place with two other strips. "That'll take care of you until we can get you to a hospital."

The Leader checked his skin pouch of darts and foreshafts, picked up his atl-atl, and levered himself to a standing position. "I'm not going to a hospital, not until you capture Bob James. I'll ride with you."

"The hell you—" began Lindman.

"I know where he's going, and I understand how he thinks. Without me, he'll escape."

"Why, you arrogant . . . "

The Leader strolled majestically toward the jeep, his left arm held stiffly across his chest. "We don't have the time for name calling, Sheriff Lindman."

"For God's sake, Lindman, drop it!" commanded Charles as he climbed into the driver's seat and waited impatiently as the Leader climbed into the back seat, followed by Polanski.

Lindman spoke, the expression on his face as forboding as Mount Capulin's crater. "All right, where's he going?"

"Capulin. I think consciously he intends to steal a car."

"Why didn't he take this jeep, or steal one of the other cars at the hotel?" asked Polanski.

"I had his keys," said Charles. "And I think even our deaf, dumb, and blind troopers might have heard a car being started. But why wouldn't he go to Folsom?"

The Leader stared at Capulin, profiled against the starlit sky. "He ran to the nearest object of his obsession."

Lindman's first comment contained four letters. "What does that mean in plain English?"

Charles shifted into the lowest gear, the ground was progressively rougher as they came closer to the crater. "Obsession was the motive. Bob James had a passion for archeology that exceeded any sexual obsession, and he wished to gain the respect of the profession by his discovery of the new Folsom Man artifacts at the dig. Armijo ridiculed his passion and was going to deny him his gain by refusing to give him any credit for his discoveries. It was all there in the journals."

Lindman sat shaking his head as if he couldn't believe what he was hearing. "Just when did you figure all this out?"

Charles slowed the jeep. The ground was becoming increasingly more rugged the closer they came to Capulin. "When David said Dr. Hagan searched Armijo's room and didn't find the journals. That explanation made much more sense than our theorizing that they didn't have time to search, or that David was too upset. Once I accepted that, I asked myself who would replace them. Not Dr. Hagan and not David. Raul didn't have them, and Mary James would never do anything to jeopardize David Lessing. That left Bob James."

"Not thirty minutes ago you had Lessing nailed to the wall with a motive an idiot could understand, even had physical evidence to back up your theory, now you're giving me some nonsense it's gonna take a psychiatrist to explain to a jury. And speaking of explaining, just how do you explain Bob James getting back in the hotel after he hit you and went out that window and down the tree? He didn't follow his wife in, because David would've seen him, and he didn't come in later because David was downstairs calling me, and again would've seen him. So just how did he manage it?"

Charles swerved to avoid a lava boulder. "He didn't go down the tree; he went up the tree and through a third story window. We didn't think of that because the third story isn't used, but the staircase is behind a door just across the hall from Bob James's bedroom. While his wife, David, and Dr. Hagan are finding me, he opens the door, takes two steps, and he's in his own bedroom."

"But where did David Lessing go when he left the hotel, if he wasn't climbing down that tree?" demanded Lindman.

"He went to tell the Leader I was a sheriff. That's why

184

you weren't surprised when Lindman introduced me, wasn't it?" Charles asked the Leader.

"Your guesses are all correct," said the Leader, his voice still weak.

"Why the hell didn't you tell us that?" asked Lindman, his question preceded by vicious oath.

"He didn't know I'd been assaulted, and David didn't have a chance to tell him. We were watching him and Dr. Hagan both from last night on—" A loud clang cut Charles's explanations short as a bullet ricocheted off the metal frame of the windshield. He swerved behind a lava squeeze-up "Everybody out!" he yelled as he cut the motor and jumped out to land rolling on the ground.

"Damn it! Now he's shooting at me!" Lindman's voice held a mixture of incredulity and anger as he peered around the edge of the squeeze-up. "Where the hell did he get that rifle, anyway? If he carried it out of the hotel with him, I'll have that trooper's guts for garters."

"I believe your car is the one with the smashed left fender?" The Leader's voice held a note of inquiry.

Lindman jerked around and glared at the Leader. "Yeah, Polanski sideswiped an overpass on the way back from Albuquerque."

"Did your car have a gun in a holster arrangement in the door?"

"Yeah. What about it?"

"When I left the hotel your car door was open and the gun was gone. The logical conclusion is that Bob James stole it"

Charles was awed by the range of Lindman's profanity. Being fluent in only two of Lindman's three languages, he couldn't be absolutely certain, but he was fairly sure that the Clayton sheriff didn't repeat a single phrase in five minutes of nonstop cursing.

"And on top of shooting at me with my own gun, he's

got us pinned down. Damn it, Matthews, couldn't you have found a bigger chunk of lava? This piece ain't much bigger than my desk."

"That bullet hit on my side of the jeep. I wasn't interested in taking the time to measure the damn rocks."

"Where are those state policemen?" asked Polanski between sneezes. "Sorry, but it's lying in all this dead grass."

Lindman jerked his head down and flattened himself on the ground as a bullet whined by, chipping a piece of lava on its way. He twisted around and looked back at the way they'd come. "Looks like they're pinned down about a hundred yards back." He raised his voice to a loud bellow. "One of you men get on the radio and call for help!"

"Johnson tried, sir. He got shot in the leg, and we're out of range anyway."

"Then keep him pinned down. They'll hear the shooting at the hotel and call for help. Or the rangers will hear it." Lindman twisted back around and squeezed off a shot in the general direction of Capulin. "The way my luck's been running those boys back there couldn't hit a privy if they were sitting in it."

"I don't believe you can do much better with your gun, Sheriff Lindman," the Leader remarked. "Handguns aren't very accurate at this range."

"It makes me feel better, and maybe I'll get lucky," snarled Lindman.

Charles stripped off his coat and shivered, shirtless, in the cold air. "I'm going after him."

"The hell you say," said Lindman, pushing himself up and crawling over to Charles. "He'll kill you the minute you stand up."

"I'm not standing up," said Charles matter-of-factly. "I'm crawling."

186

"I don't care if you hop like a bunny rabbit, he'll spot you and drill a hole right through that handsome head. He's a damn good shot in case you hadn't noticed."

"Loan me your gun," said Charles, crawling under the jeep.

"Where's yours?"

"I don't carry one," he replied, concentrating more on draining the oil from the jeep than listening to Lindman. Mixing the greasy black oil with dirt, he rubbed the concoction on his face and chest, feeling as if he were going on night patrol in Vietnam. He felt the same cold, shaky sensation in his belly; the same dryness in his mouth; the same icy detachment from his gentler emotions. He also felt the same burst of adrenaline that created a feeling of invincibility. *Which is stupid,* he thought wryly as he touched the band of scar tissue that crossed his abdomen and ended near his spine. He was far from invincible.

He scooted out from under the jeep and into the middle of Lindman's low-voiced tirade.... "And you're still my deputy, not some wild eyed Texas sheriff, and any time you think I'm gonna let my deputy get shot up so the county'll have to pay a big hospital bill, you're not dealing with a full deck. So you just wipe that oil off your face and hunker down here in the dirt with the rest of us until the cavalry gets here."

Charles interrupted him. "How much ammunition do you have in your car, Lindman?"

"Uh? A box, maybe two."

"Bob James won't surrender; he'll sit up on the side of Capulin and pick us off one by one until he runs out of ammunition. He's got the high ground, Lindman. It'd take an army to get him down, and you'd have casualties, more than you want to live with. One man has a better chance of sneaking up the crater than an army. "Give me your gun, Lindman."

Lindman looked at Charles, then down at his gun. "It's my county, Matthews, my job."

"Actually, as an FBI agent, it's my job," said Polanski with a sneeze.

"You couldn't sneak up on a deaf jackrabbit, Polanski," said Lindman.

"I spent two years in Vietnam, most of it crawling around on my belly. I can make it," said Charles, his voice impatient. Too much waiting, too much arguing. The adrenaline was seeping away, leaving him feeling tired and shaky and unsure of himself, which was damn dangerous. Crawling on your belly after someone who would as soon shoot you as look at you was not the time to feel unsure.

Lindman's voice sounded apologetic. "I sure hope you're good, Matthews, 'cause you've only got three bullets."

"What the hell are you talking about?"

"I'm out of ammunition! James took all I had out of the car. I don't end up in a lot of gun battles; I don't carry an extra box of shells, and my gun belt doesn't hold many rounds. What do you think I am? Some TV cop that gets thirty-seven shots out of a six-shot revolver? I'm just a county sheriff that arrests some drunks on Saturday night, breaks up a knife fight every now and then. I don't think I've fired a shot in the line of duty in two years or more. Until tonight. Anyway, you've got three shots."

Polanski sneezed. "You can take my gun. It's a .38."

Charles smiled at the FBI agent. He'd seen suspects in Dallas run with two or more .38 slugs in them.

"No, thanks, Polanski," he said. "You'll need a gun down here."

He accepted Lindman's gun belt and strapped it around his waist when the Leader grasped his arm. "Take the atl-atl, Sheriff Matthews. If you should miss with the gun, it is fully as lethal up to three hundred feet. He won't move with a dart point in his shoulder or leg either."

Charles swallowed. "No. I might kill him, and I can't risk that."

"And you will not bring him down otherwise," said the Leader, looking toward Capulin.

"And I can't do otherwise than try," said Charles, taking a deep breath. Saluting Lindman and Polanski with a casual movement of his hand, he moved away from the squeeze-up, crawling on his belly in the best military tradition.

22

HE FELT EXPOSED. He'd forgotten that sensation from his night patrols in Vietnam, the feeling that your body was twice as large as it actually was. By keeping flat on his belly, the high clumps of dead grass and chunks of lava boulders, as well as the short wizened bushes, provided enough cover. He hoped. It didn't help that Bob James was near the top of the rim and was looking down on him. He heard Polanski's .38 and risked a glance at the volcano. He heard the rifle's crack and the flash of light from the barrel. James was now on the rim.

Crawling more quickly, he moved from lava block to lava block, ignoring the scratches and tiny cuts inflicted on his chest and stomach by the weeds, bushes, and small pebbles. He felt a warm liquid trickle down his chest and debated with himself as to whether it was blood or sweat. It didn't matter; he'd have lost some of both before the night was over.

He reached the foot of Capulin and rolled over on his back. He was panting, his chest heaving in an attempt to inhale enough air. Damn it, what was the matter with him? The altitude! The altitude was higher, cutting his body's efficiency because he wasn't used to it. Could he make it to the top?

He gritted his teeth and rolled back over onto his belly. He'd make it, by God, he'd make it for everyone: for Raul, for David Lessing, for Lindman and Polanski, pinned down and vulnerable.

The edge of the sun was just visible on the horizon,

its light soft and blood-red. It caught the rim of the volcano and Charles risked a glance upward. Only a hundred or so more feet to the top. He'd barely made it across the road that spiraled upward to the crater rim while there was darkness enough for cover. He was bleeding from a hundred scratches and sweat rolled into his eyes, making him blink rapidly. He was tired, and the cut on his thigh was bleeding again, but he crawled on, his back and arms one continuous ache.

When he reached the narrow asphalt path that circled the rim, he stopped and cautiously raised his head to look both ways. He saw no trace of Bob James and silently wiggled on to the path and pushed himself up to a crouching position. He pulled Lindman's gun from the holster, its weight and contours familiar. He peered along the path and silently moved eastward in the direction of the last shot. The path swerved around a gnarled pinyon pine and he swung wide to one side to see beyond its crooked, spindly branches. A bullet sang through the space he'd occupied a split second before, and he hit the ground and rolled off the path to crouch behind a boulder.

"Matthews!" Bob James's voice was a shrill sound that echoed off the sides of the crater. "Matthews, I know you're there."

Charles looked at the gun in his hand. Three bullets! And how many rounds did Bob James have left? Twenty? Fifty? A bookmaker wouldn't give very good odds on his chances of making it out of this. "James! Give it up! We'll have an army up here in a few hours, and we'll take you in. There's no way you can escape."

He waited a few seconds, then peered around the boulder. This time a bullet creased his forehead. He jerked back and felt the wound. Just a nick, more blood than damage, but his stomach heaved in reaction. He swallowed to control the nausea and tried to estimate where James was. He recalled the quick glimpse he'd had of the trail. It curved, then climbed for twenty or so feet. At the top of the incline was another large boulder just off the path. That's where Bob James must be.

Charles looked backward. If he could crawl backward down the side of the crater for a few feet, then angle sideways around it, it might be possible to come up behind him. If he could do it silently through all the brush. But first give Bob James something to consider. "Bob, you have two ways to come out of this crater: dead or alive. Dead, you'll never dig artifacts again, never even touch one. But alive, there's hope."

"Sure there is, Matthews," answered James, his voice still distorted sounding, but even the distortion couldn't disguise the bitterness. "I can hope to spend the rest of my life in a cage. That's no way for a man to live."

"A man doesn't stab a young girl in the back, either," said Charles with some bitterness of his own.

"I didn't really want to do that, but I didn't have a choice. She should've stayed in that damn circle."

"Why didn't you kill her that night?" asked Charles. "Why did you wait?" He began edging slowly backward, then sideways, a zigzag course that took advantage of boulders, heavy brush, anything that provided cover.

"Actually," began James in a conversational tone, "I didn't realize she'd seen me, not until yesterday morning, when you were questioning the Leader. I knew I had to kill her; I couldn't chance her talking, but I couldn't figure out a way to get away from the dig to do it. Then the Leader stole my jeep, and we found the skeleton, and Dr. Hagan finally decided to call in a team. I volunteered to go back and call. It was damn bad luck that Lessing and Raul went, too. But I lost them. I know this country like the back of my hand, and I just took off and lost them. As soon as they were out of sight, I headed toward the cave. As it turned out, Faith came running out of the underbrush, breathing hard and as wild-eyed as a coyote running from the hunter. I'd stolen one of those kid's flint knives, and I just chased her down and grabbed her. I dragged her behind a lava boulder when I heard Raul yell, and I waited until he was at the edge of the clearing, stabbed her, and pushed her out almost in front of him. She was struggling so hard that I missed my angle, and she didn't die immediately. That worked for the best though, because Raul stopped to try to help her instead of chasing me."

Charles let Bob James's words wash over him and tried not to visualize what he was describing. A flash of light distracted his thoughts, and he stopped abruptly, parallel to the large boulder. Bob James was lying almost on top of it, looking toward Charles's erstwhile shelter. Charles propped himself up on his elbows, holding his gun in one fist which he rested in the palm of his other hand. He sighted carefully, drew a breath, and fired. There was a cry, and Bob James rolled from sight.

Charles rose to a crouch and stumbled up the hill, tripping on a small rock and sprawling on his belly across the path. The crack of the rifle at close range and the horrible buzzing sound of a near miss sent him rolling toward the interior of the crater and its luxurious brush. He caught a movement out of the corner of his eye, snapped off a quick shot, then cursed himself. He had one round left.

"You're a lousy shot, Matthews." Bob James's voice mocked him. "Less than ten yards and you didn't kill me."

Charles stayed silent. He wasn't hiding behind a boulder this time, and he couldn't allow himself the luxury of replying to James and giving away his position. Somehow he doubted that a chokecherry bush would deflect a bullet.

"Did you know I can hit a target the size of a nickel

from ten yards with an atl-atl? And you can't even use a gun sight and hit something as big as a man."

Charles moved his arms an inch at a time until again he was resting his hand holding the gun in the palm of his other hand. He searched the area from which James's voice was coming. One round left. He must see his target before firing.

"You still alive, Matthews, and just playing possum? I think you are. You've been lucky, keeping your head down, never giving me much of a target. You're good at it; must be the war. Now Armijo made a good target. He was between me and the fire and I could see him fine."

Charles glanced away from the direction of James's voice. He'd learned to do that. Sometimes you caught movement more easily using your peripheral vision, rather than looking at something directly.

Bob James's voice continued. He sounded more calm, as if he and Charles were having coffee together and discussing the morning headlines. "You're pretty good at sneaking up on a fellow, too. I almost didn't hear you. Not like Lessing. He sounded like a herd of buffalo coming down the side of the crater. He passed within a yard of me, that's how I knew it was him. It's funny when you think about it, isn't it, Matthews? Lessing and I were both in that crater to murder Armijo. Shows you how much the man needed killing."

There was a blur of movement to Charles's left and twenty yards away. Quickly he focused on it. Bob James's khaki-colored clothes were almost impossible to detect, as camouflage would be. Charles's eyes were burning with strain when he finally located what he believed was the older's man's torso and head. Carefully he aimed for a head shot. He started to squeeze the trigger, then hesitated as he thought of just how much damage a .357 could do to a human skull. His gun dipped as he aimed for a shoulder instead and just at that instant the rising sun reflected off the metal barrel into his eyes. His finger jerked, and the sound of the shot echoed.

There was another cry and then a string of curses that dissolved into laughter. "You missed me again, Matthews."

Charles licked his lips, tasting the mixture of oil and sweat on his skin. He tightened his grip on his gun and stealthily crawled forward, his body feeling nine feet long and three feet thick. He was out of ammunition, totally vulnerable except for an empty gun, and that was only useful if he could get close enough to use it as a club. He didn't think he'd be able to get that close.

He stopped and pressed his forehead against the ground. He didn't want to die, not now and not like this, shot like a trapped animal by a crazy man. His fist curled up, his fingers digging into the loose topsoil, and he looked up again. He *would* live, by God; he'd live to watch the brilliant red and orange and yellow Panhandle sunsets that covered the whole western sky, live to see the cottonwoods along the Canadian River turn gold in the autumn. But most of all he'd live to see Angie again and this time there'd be no ghosts between them.

"Matthews." The voice was close and Charles froze. "Matthews, if you'd stayed away, everything would have been all right. But you had to stir things up, start asking questions. I've lost everything because of you." There was silence for a moment, then Bob James continued, his voice a monotone. "I've even lost my wife, now that she knows I killed Armijo; I drugged her that night. She didn't know.

His laugh was also a monotone, and Charles felt the fine hairs on his arms and the back of his neck stiffen. "I drugged her herbal tea, Matthews. Can you see the humor? I added another herb to her damn herbal tea. She never would have known about Armijo if you hadn't come. I had to put those journals back so you'd suspect

Lessing, and that's when I had trouble. I had to lie about the pass key; I said we didn't have one and Mary knew we did. But she was loyal, stuck right in there with me and backed me up. Until I had to kill Faith. That was your fault too, Matthews. If you hadn't pestered her, she'd probably have forgotten what she saw by next week."

Charles didn't move, hardly breathed, and hoped his heartbeat wasn't as loud as it sounded to him. He had to stay hidden until he was a little closer to Bob James, close enough to knock him out. The man was completely mad, beyond the reach of reason. One more murder would mean nothing to him.

"I wish I had a beer. Wouldn't you like to have a beer, Matthews? No, I guess not; you're not a beer drinker. You know what you are? A damn Boy Scout. Had to come to help your friend, didn't you? Had to mess in something that wasn't any of your business. You want to know why I really want to kill you?" There was a sharp click as he loaded another round into the rifle chamber. "I want to kill you because you cost me the dig. Did you hear that, Matthews? You cost me the dig! That was *my* skeleton we found yesterday. Mine! Everybody would have heard about it. I'd have been in the newspapers, on TV! I could have written a book about the dig! Everybody would have heard about Bob James!" A volley of shots echoed as he fired round after round at the spot where Charles had been.

Echoes rolled like thunder around the crater, and Charles crawled forward under the cover of the sound, ignoring the stinging pain from new scratches and cuts on his chest and arms. He stopped and peered through a screen of Gambel oak at his quarry stretched out flat behind a chunk of lava. Bob James's shirt was tied around his shoulder, and blood flowed down his back in an irregular pattern that looked almost like a child's connect-the-dot picture as it trickled among the freckles. Blood clotted his neck and the side of his head where a bullet had notched his ear. Charles grimaced. Not even a .357 would stop a man if you couldn't hit anything more solid than the top of his shoulder and his ear.

"Matthews, you bastard! Have I got you yet?" James raised up to look over the lava. "Matthews! Where are you?"

Charles rose to a crouch, tensing his thigh muscles. "Right here, James!" he yelled as he sprang forward, his empty gun raised like a club.

Bob James twisted sideways with the rapidity of a snake, and the barrel of Charles's gun barely grazed his head. Dropping his worthless gun, Charles grabbed for the smaller man's rifle and felt his oily, sweaty hands slip harmlessly off the barrel.

"Missed me, you bastard!" yelled James as he used the rifle butt like an extra elbow, jabbing Charles in the side.

Charles caught his breath at the explosion of pain in the left side of his body. *Ribs,* he thought numbly as he grabbed James's arm, digging his fingers into the flesh in desperation. The rifle! He had to force James to drop the rifle. And soon. Between the pain in his side forcing him to breath in shallow gasps, and the oxygen-poor air at this altitude, he felt as though he were suffocating. A second later the rifle rammed into his belly, and he lost what little air he had left. He felt James twist loose, and he tried to roll after him, anything but being shot lying on the ground gaping like a fish out of water.

"Almost got me," panted James, smashing the rifle butt into Charles's shoulder, then rolling several feet before staggering to his feet. "But almost isn't good enough."

He pointed the rifle at Charles, his lips stretched over

his teeth like a feral animal. "Got any last words, Matthews, or can't you talk?"

His maniacal laughter bounced off the rim of the crater. It was the last sound he ever made. The Folsom projectile point ripped through his body and erupted through his chest. He dropped his rifle and gaped at the projectile, then looked at Charles in silent resignation before his body crumbled and his eyes glazed over in death.

Charles rose to one knee, then slumped back against the lava boulder that had been Bob James's last shelter. He held his side and drew a deep breath in spite of the pain. "Why?" he yelled at the skin-clad figure making his way slowly down the side of the crater.

The Leader leaned heavily on his atl-atl as though it were a cane and with careful steps he walked the last few feet toward Charles. He looked at Bob James's body, and something like regret flashed across his black eyes. He sank down beside Charles and leaned back against the boulder. "It's ended where it all began: in the crater." He coughed and a froth of blood flecked his lips. "You were right when you said I was responsible for the murders. I accept responsibility for forging this chain of death, and I accept responsibility for breaking it."

"You didn't have that right," replied Charles, his face as harsh as his voice.

The Leader glanced at him. "You are a civilized man, Sheriff Matthews, a man of abstract law and rules, of judges in black robes and twelve good men and true. I am not. And neither was Bob James," he said, nodding at the crumbled body. "Otherwise we would never have killed at all."

He broke off to cough again, this time bringing up bright red blood. He shrugged off Charles's hand and waved him away. "I may not be civilized, but I recognize

198

civilization's penalties for breaking its laws, and I choose my own method of payment."

"We'll argue about that later. Right now we have to get you to a hospital."

The Leader shook his head. "It's too late. Bob James shot me through the chest, not the shoulder. I'm dying, and I don't choose to do anything about it."

"This is one choice you're not going to make," said Charles grimly as he pushed himself up.

The Leader smiled, a surprisingly kind smile that stunned Charles. "Save your compassion for the ones who need it." He gripped Charles's hand. "Save it for David Lessing and Dr. Hagan and Mary James."

He looked out over the crater. "It's a fitting place to die, a primitive, uncivilized place. Perfect for a primitive, uncivilized man."

He raised his voice in a wordless chant and heard it answered in echoes off the crater rim as he died, almost as if a population of spirits were welcoming him into their world. Then there was no noise but the wind rustling through the bushes like scores of footsteps marching slowly in a funeral procession. Charles raised his hand in a silent farewell, then kept company with the dead.

EPILOGUE

"Matthews!"

Lindman's voice was a welcome reality and Charles sat up and waved one arm. "Over here," he yelled.

Lindman and Polanski both showed the effects of a night spent huddling in the dirt behind a lava squeeze-up. Both were dirty, rumpled, tired, and in Lindman's case, badly in need of a shave. Polanski clutched his inevitable handkerchief, now a tattletale grey, and looked like a seedy businessman on the edge of bankruptcy rather than a spit and polish FBI agent.

"Good God almighty!" exclaimed Lindman as he stood over Bob James's body. "Skewered him."

He hunkered down by the Leader's body and pulled the antelope hide cloak off. He peeled off the blood-soaked pad and examined the wound. "Lung shot; probably bled to death. I don't know how the hell he ever climbed up here with that kind of wound."

He took his Stetson off and rubbed his arm across his forehead. "He got away from us. Polanski and I were trying to watch you, and he sneaked off in the dark. The man moved like a ghost."

"He saved my life," said Charles, closing his eyes.

"I doubt if that was his intention," remarked Polanski, looking a little green around the mouth as he stared at the wooden main shaft protruding from Bob James's chest.

"I'll give him the benefit of the doubt," said Charles as he began to struggle to his feet.

Lindman put his hat back on and offered Charles a hand. "I guess we'd better get back to the hotel. I'll call my medical investigator. Not that there's much to investigate. Bob James shot the Leader and the Leader, uh, speared him. I don't think there'll be any argument about who's guilty this time." He looked at Charles. "You look like hell, Matthews."

Charles let Lindman pull him up. "I'm resigning, Lindman." He fumbled in his pocket until he found his billfold and removed the deputy's badge. "I guess I'm a coward, but I can't face any more waste."

"What are you referring to?" asked Polanski, turning aside to sneeze.

Charles looked at Lindman. "Lessing, Dr. Hagan, and Mary James. There are always lives wasted in a murder case other than the actual victim, Polanski. Sometimes I think the victim is the lucky one; he misses all the misery of the survivors."

Lindman nodded, his face somber. "They interfered with a murder investigation at the very least. Technically, you might even consider them accessories to murder."

Polanski studied his handkerchief as if he'd never seen it before. "That's true," he agreed reluctantly.

Lindman stuck his hands in his pockets and studied the two dead bodies. "Armijo, Faith, Bob James, the Leader; that's four victims. I sure hate to add three more to the toll."

"No, there is another," said Charles quietly. "The dig."

Lindman frowned. "The dig? What are you talking about, Matthews?"

"If you arrest Lessing and Dr. Hagan, then everyone will know they salted the dig. No one will believe the skeleton and those Folsom points are authentic. The most important find since the original Folsom site won't be investigated. We'll lose knowledge, Lindman."

"How important can an old skeleton be?" demanded Lindman.

"I don't know," replied Charles. "Do you?"

Lindman looked out over the crater. "But I can't just let them walk. I can't let somebody break the law without any punishment at all."

"Mary James will punish herself," said Charles, thinking of the woman's tortured face. "I don't think even prison would be as severe as what she'll do to herself."

"There's still Lessing and Dr. Hagan," said Lindman, turning back to meet Charles's eyes. "I'm open to suggestions."

"Do you consider them a danger to society?"

Lindman cocked an eyebrow. "If you're asking me if I think they might get involved in some other hairbrained scheme again, the answer's no. A good attorney could claim they were brainwashed and I'm not so sure but what that's true. The Leader could've brainwashed damn near anybody."

"It's too bad you can't just run them out of town, I believe the expression is," said Polanski.

Charles reached out and shook the agent's hand. "Polanski, you're brilliant."

"Now wait a minute," interrupted Lindman. "I can't take them to the Union County line and tell them never to come back."

"Deny them the dig," said Charles urgently. "Make them turn it over to another archeological team to investigate. Forbid them to even go near it under threat of revealing they salted it with artifacts in the first place."

"That's blackmail!" said Lindman, but he looked thoughtful.

Charles drew a deep breath and pain sliced across his chest. He felt light-headed and wished he could just walk away, get into his car, drive back to Crawford County and Angie, and forget all about New Mexico and Capulin and the Folsom Man. But he couldn't. The dig was the only good thing to come out of all this, the only balance to the lies and the hatred and the deaths. It must not be wasted.

"Yes, technically it is blackmail," he agreed; "it's against the letter of the law. And we aren't the lawmakers; we are the law enforcers. We haven't the right to interpret the law, that's for the courts to do. We're Pharisees of society, Lindman, strict observers of custom. Not so very many years ago our kind arrested starving men for stealing a loaf of bread and watched them hang. I wonder how many lives were wasted before life was considered more important than a loaf of bread?"

He pressed his arm against his side to try to ease the pain. "I can't be a Pharisee anymore; I can't be a part of sending a scared kid, an old man, and a pitiful woman to prison."

Lindman grinned. "You're a tough bastard, Matthews. I think Dr. Hagan and Lessing would rather go to jail than give up that dig. A judge and jury couldn't come up with a worse punishment. What do you think, Polanski?" he asked the inspector.

Polanski sneezed. "I think I'm a very bad Pharisee." He wiped his nose. "Do you think we can go back to the hotel now? All this brush is terrible for my allergies."

If you have enjoyed this book and would like to
receive details of other Walker mystery titles, please
write to:

Mystery Editor
Walker and Company
720 Fifth Avenue
New York, NY 10019